Rectified

The Recollection

Kris Michael McKenna

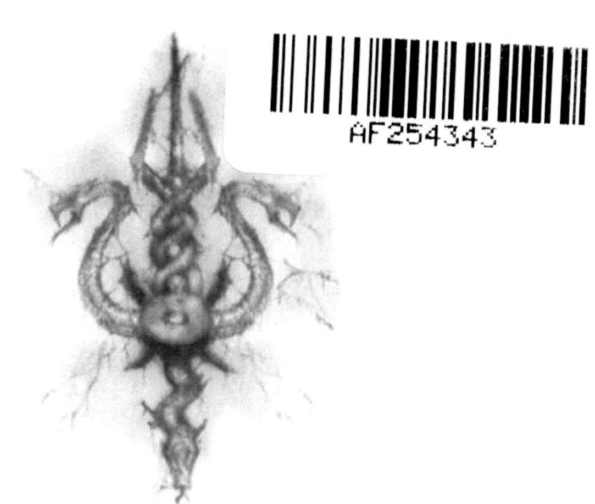

PP

PUBLISHING PLACE LLC
www.publishingplace.net

PP

Rectified: The Recollection | by Kris Michael McKenna

ISBN: 978-1-969343-13-1 (*Paperback*)

LCCN: 2025927466

Printed & Published in the United States of America, Publishing Place LLC, Skowhegan, Maine,

2nd Edition 2026.

www.publishingplace.net

Author's Note

Rectified: The Recollection began as a short experimental film and was adapted to a feature film screenplay written by Kris Michael McKenna and Kristian Michael Hickman between 2009-2010 and registered with the Writers Guild of America (Registration #VQCA2D8B3AB1). The screenplay was developed as part of a complete film package including the graphic novel adaptation, musical attachment by Jesper Kyd, and production plans for what was envisioned as a supernatural thriller exploring the century-long consequences of binding a priest to a demon.

This novel represents a complete adaptation of that screenplay into traditional prose fiction. While every scene, character, and plot beat remains faithful to the original script, the novel form allows for expanded internal perspectives, atmospheric detail, and the kind of slow-burn supernatural dread that only literary fiction can provide.

The story you're about to read is the same one we wrote for the screen—complete with its detective noir atmosphere, ancient cult conspiracy, and that final moment when a bound soul remembers who he truly was. But now you'll experience it the way novels let us experience stories: from the inside out, with full access to the thoughts, fears, and impossible choices of everyone caught in a war that began a hundred years ago.

Welcome to Detroit, 2019. July 15th. Where the past is about to collide with the present in fire and ash.

—Kris Michael McKenna, 2026

CONTENTS

THE RECTIFIER
DESIGN BY | BRIAN WADE

PROLOGUE

July 14th, 2019

The photographs lay scattered across the cathedral floor like accusations.

Father Paul's hands trembled as he bent to pick one up. His breath caught. The image showed a young girl—maybe nine years old—sitting on a bed. Blonde hair. Frightened eyes. And sitting next to her, his arm around her shoulders, was a younger version of himself.

"No, please... You don't understand!"

His voice echoed through the empty cathedral. Saint Anthony's had stood for over a century, weathering Detroit's rise and fall, bearing witness to countless confessions and prayers and desperate pleas for salvation. Tonight it would witness something else entirely.

Father Paul followed the trail of photographs up the center aisle toward the altar, picking them up as he went. Each one the same scene.

Different angles. Different moments. All damning in their implication despite their innocence.

"These aren't what they seem," he whispered to the shadows. "She needed protection. I was trying to help her. Trying to prepare her for—"

A loud slam behind him.

Father Paul spun around.

The heavy oak doors had closed. Standing within the shadows near the entrance was a large, cloaked figure. Its eyes glowed with golden fire.

"I... I..." Father Paul backed toward the altar, photographs falling from his hands.

The figure moved up the center aisle with deliberate purpose. Each step measured. Inevitable. The glow of its eyes illuminated nothing except the promise of what was coming.

Father Paul reached the altar and pressed his back against it. His mind raced through prayers, through Latin passages he'd memorized over decades of service, through the rituals he'd studied in secret for this very possibility.

But none of them would help him now.

The figure stopped a few feet away. Close enough that Father Paul could feel the heat radiating from it. Could see the way the air shimmered around its massive frame.

"Please," Father Paul said. "She's not ready yet. I need more time. Just a few more months. She needs to understand what's at stake. What she'll have to—"

All the candles in the cathedral blew out simultaneously.

Darkness swallowed the space except for those burning golden eyes.

Father Paul opened his mouth to scream, to pray, to plead.

Heat.

Incredible heat.

And then nothing.

***

Rain hammered the Detroit streets with biblical intensity. Christy Harris ran through the downpour toward her car, designer heels splashing through puddles, her thousand-dollar dress already soaked through and ruined.

The benefit dinner had run late. Her mother—Senator Belinda Harris—had insisted she stay for the final speech, the photo opportunities, the networking that defined their family's existence. Politics and power and carefully constructed public images.

Christy just wanted to go home.

She fumbled with her keys in the alley behind Mickey's Tavern. The lot was poorly lit, water pooling in the broken pavement, steam rising from manhole covers. Detroit at night. Beautiful and broken and dangerous.

Two silhouettes lurked in the distance.

She looked over at them. Fumbled more with the keys. They fell into a puddle.

"Shit."

She bent quickly, grabbed them, looked up.

The men were gone.

Something grabbed her from behind—rough hands, violent intent, dragging her deeper into the alley past sleeping bums who wouldn't meet her eyes.

"Fuck off and mind your business," one of her attackers growled.

The other flashed a gun. The bums skulked away.

Christy fought. Kicked. Screamed. But there were two of them and they were strong and practiced and determined. They tore at her clothing, groped her, pushed her down into the filthy alley water.

"Don't fight it! You got it coming looking the way you do." She screamed again. One of them hit her. Hard. Her vision swam. She stopped fighting.

This is how I die, she thought. In an alley. Like trash. Like my life meant nothing.

Somewhere above her, seated on a fire escape in the shadows, a large figure watched. Rain dripped off his hat. Steam rose from his body. His eyes glowed golden in the darkness.

He'd been watching her for weeks. Following her. Protecting her without understanding why. Something about her face triggered memories he didn't know he had. Sparked emotions in a heart that shouldn't be capable of emotion.

Carlos—the one undoing his pants—looked up and saw him.

The Rectifier wiped his mouth and dropped to the ground. The fire escape sprang back up with a metallic shriek.

He walked toward them. His glowing eyes narrowed.

Carlos pulled a knife "Don't you pieces of shit listen?" brandishing the handle like a professional knife-fighter "I told you get the fuck out of here!"

The Rectifier said nothing.

"Hey, I'm talking to you. What, you like to watch or something? Get the fuck out of here... or I'm gonna cut you up, asshole!"

He didn't stop his advance. Carlos lunged. Buried the knife in the Rectifier's stomach.

The Rectifier looked down. Slowly pulled the knife out. The blade was melted, metal dripping like wax.

Carlos backed away, all bravado gone. "What the fuck..."

The Rectifier threw the handle aside and stood to his full height—easily seven feet tall, massive shoulders, hands the size of dinner plates. He dwarfed Carlos.

"Holy s-shit..." Freddy's jaw dropped.

Carlos tried to run. The Rectifier grabbed the back of his neck, pressed him against the wall. Carlos's feet dangled and kicked uselessly.

The Rectifier's hand burned through Carlos's neck. Cauterized. Severed.

Carlos's head fell to the ground with a wet thud.

Freddy ran screaming into the night.

The Rectifier walked to Christy, who was struggling to move away despite her injuries. He bent down and looked at her.

Christy's head was tilted down, shaking, face hidden.

The Rectifier grabbed her arms gently—gently for him, at least—and lifted her like a rag doll. He stared into her face. A face stared back, a memory...

A faded memory of Fields. Sunlight. 1919. *A woman named Marybeth laughing, spinning in tall grass, her face turned up toward the sky. The same face. The same eyes. The memory of being human. Of being in love. Of being Father Josef Willem before everything went wrong.*

The Rectifier confused about his purpose. The temporary release causing interference. The came back to his reality, his prison.

He unleashed his grasp on the sleeves of Christy's leather coat that were beginning to smoke where he held her. She flopped to the ground, pulled off the smoking coat, threw it near her shoes in a puddle.

The Rectifier looked agitated. This woman had sparked something. A lost memory. A connection he didn't understand but couldn't ignore.

Christy huddled in a fetal position, too terrified to look at the thing that had saved her life.

The Rectifier walked away into the rain and darkness, leaving her alive, leaving Carlos's headless body cooling in the alley, leaving questions that would lead a detective named Leland Jamo into a conspiracy spanning one-hundred years.

The night of July 14th, 2019.

Twenty-four hours before everything would change.

Twenty-four hours before The Recollection.

The ending of one age.

The beginning of another.

And in Saint Anthony's Cathedral, Father Paul's body hung from a cross, gutted and displayed as a warning to anyone who might interfere with plans a century in the making.

The Knights of Flauros were moving.

The ritual was nearly ready.

All the pieces were in place.

Tomorrow—July 15th, the anniversary of Father Willem's transformation—the binding would be renewed.

Or it would be broken. Or something else entirely.

One way or another.

The hundred-year cycle would end.

CHAPTER 1
FATHER PAUL

The cathedral stood like a monument to forgotten promises in Detroit's East Side, its Gothic spires cutting into the winter sky like accusing fingers. Saint Anthony's had weathered seventy years of the city's slow decline—survived the riots, the white flight, the economic collapse that left whole neighborhoods to rot. The stone walls had absorbed decades of prayers and confessions, hope and despair in equal measure. Tonight, they would absorb something else entirely.

Father Paul moved through the pews with the careful deliberation of a man who knew every creak in the floorboards, every draft that whistled through the aging structure. At fifty-three, he carried himself with the humble authority of someone who had dedicated half his life to this parish, to these people. His graying hair caught the amber light from the votive candles as he bent to retrieve a forgotten hymnal from beneath a pew.

The church settled around him with familiar groans—old timber adjusting to the temperature drop outside, radiators ticking as they cooled for the night. He'd learned to read these sounds like a second language, could distinguish between the building's normal complaints and anything unusual.

Everything seemed normal tonight.

He moved down the center aisle, picking up the detritus of evening mass—a forgotten pair of reading glasses here, a printed psalm there. When he found the glasses in the third pew from the back, he smiled despite himself.

"Mr. Naughton," he whispered to the empty church, slipping the glasses into his breast pocket. The old man forgot them at least once a month. Father Paul would return them tomorrow, as always, enduring the same embarrassed gratitude, the same promise that it wouldn't happen again.

These small rituals gave his life structure, meaning. Tending his flock, even in the smallest ways.

The main doors loomed before him, heavy oak reinforced with iron bands installed during the riots of '67. He ran his hand along the wood—smooth in some places, scarred in others—and tested the locks. Both deadbolts slid home with satisfying clicks. The cathedral was secure.

Father Paul turned back toward the altar, taking in the vast space one last time before retiring for the night. The votive candles flickered in their red glass holders, casting dancing shadows across the stations of the cross that lined the walls. Saint Anthony himself gazed down from the stained glass above the altar, his painted expression benevolent and serene.

Tomorrow would bring another Sunday, another opportunity to guide souls toward salvation. Father Paul felt the familiar weight of that responsibility, comforting in its constancy.

He started down the center aisle, his leather shoes whispering against worn stone. Just a final check, then bed. He was tired—bone tired in a way that had been growing worse over the past weeks. Stress, his doctor said. Perhaps it was time to—

The sound stopped him mid-step.

A dull clunk from the direction of the doors.

Father Paul turned, his heart rate picking up slightly. Old buildings made noises, he reminded himself. Particularly in winter, when the temperature differentials stressed the materials. But this sound had been different. Deliberate, somehow. Like metal on metal.

He waited, listening.

The doors swung open.

Not quickly, not violently. They moved with an almost gentle grace, creaking on their hinges as they revealed the winter darkness beyond. Both of them, in perfect synchronization, as if pushed by invisible hands.

"Ah... Hello?" Father Paul's voice echoed in the suddenly cavernous space. His earlier sense of security evaporated like morning frost.

He stepped toward the open doors, his mind racing through rational explanations. The locks had been faulty? Someone had a key? A strong wind had—but there was no wind. The night beyond the threshold stood absolutely still.

As he approached, he noticed something that made his blood run cold.

Smoke.

Thin tendrils of it rose from the doors themselves, curling upward in the still air of the cathedral. And the handles—the solid brass handles that had graced these doors since the church's construction—were gone. In their place, only smoking holes remained, edges glowing faintly red like dying embers.

The metal had melted.

Father Paul's throat constricted. His hands, usually so steady when raising the Eucharist or making the sign of the cross, began to tremble. Whatever had opened these doors possessed a heat intense enough to liquify brass as if it were butter.

"Uh..." His voice cracked. "We don't have anything here for you. You can take what little money we have..."

Even as he spoke the words, he knew how absurd they sounded. This wasn't a robbery. Robbers didn't melt through locks. Robbers didn't—

A sound behind him. Not quite a sigh, not quite a breath. Something else. Something that reminded him of wind through a cave mouth, or air escaping from deep within the earth. Unnatural. Wrong.

Father Paul spun around.

At his feet, leading from the doors where he stood all the way up the center aisle to the altar, lay a trail of photographs. They were arranged with deliberate precision, each one placed face-up, creating a path through the cathedral's heart.

His hands shook as he bent to pick up the first one.

The image showed a young girl, perhaps nineteen or twenty, with blonde hair and frightened eyes. She sat in what looked like a hospital bed, her arms marked with the telltale scars and bruises of intravenous drug use. Despite the damage addiction had done to her, she possessed an almost ethereal beauty—delicate features that might have graced Renaissance paintings in another life.

Father Paul knew this face. Knew it well, though he'd never seen this particular photograph.

"No," he breathed. "Please, no."

He moved to the next photograph, already knowing what he would find. The same girl, but in different circumstances. Then another. And another. Each image documented a life spiraling toward destruction, chronicling descent into darkness with clinical precision.

Father Paul followed the trail, picking up photos as he went, tears streaming down his weathered face. They showed moments private and desperate—the girl in alleyways, in seedy motel rooms, accepting money from men whose faces were deliberately obscured. Not pornography, but something worse. Evidence. Accusation.

"Please," Father Paul's voice broke. "You don't understand!"

He reached the altar and knelt, clutching the photographs to his chest like a man trying to shield a child from harm. The faces blurred through his tears, but he didn't need to see them clearly. He'd been there for some of these moments, trying to help, trying to save a soul that seemed determined to slip through his fingers.

Behind him, a sound like thunder.

The doors slammed shut.

Father Paul's head snapped around. In the darkness at the back of the cathedral, barely visible in the dim glow of votive candles, stood a figure. Massive. Cloaked in something that didn't quite move right, as if the fabric itself recoiled from what it covered.

And the eyes.

Two points of golden light in the shadow, burning with an intensity that seemed to pierce the darkness, the distance, the very air between them.

"I... I..." Father Paul struggled to form words, his tongue thick in his mouth. "I was trying to help her. I would never—"

The figure moved.

It didn't walk so much as flow up the center aisle, each step deliberate yet somehow wrong. The geometry of its movement didn't quite match human locomotion. Shadows clung to it like living things, reluctant to release their hold even when candlelight should have illuminated its features.

Father Paul scrambled backward, his feet tangling in his cassock. The altar pressed against his spine. Nowhere left to go. No escape.

"Please," he whispered. "I tried to protect her. I've always tried to protect—"

The figure stopped at the edge of the candlelight, and for one horrible moment, Father Paul saw it clearly. Not a man, though it wore a man's approximate shape. Something else. Something that had perhaps once been human but had been transformed into something terrible and magnificent and utterly merciless.

The Rectifier.

Father Paul's breath came in short gasps. Years of theological training, decades of ministering to the suffering, countless hours spent contemplating the nature of good and evil—none of it had prepared him for this moment. This being standing before him rendered all his carefully constructed understanding of the world obsolete.

He opened his mouth to pray, to beg, to say something that might reach whatever humanity might still exist within that burning gaze.

The candles in the cathedral went out simultaneously.

Darkness swallowed the church whole. In the sudden absence of light, Father Paul's other senses sharpened. He heard his own breathing, rapid and shallow. The creak of floorboards as something massive moved closer. A smell like heated metal and burning incense.

And heat. Terrible, overwhelming heat radiating from the figure that now stood directly before him.

Father Paul felt hands grasp his shoulders—hands that burned even through his cassock, through his shirt, branding his flesh with their touch. He tried to scream, but no sound emerged. The heat intensified, spreading through his body like liquid fire coursing through his veins.

In his last moments of consciousness, Father Paul's mind fragmented into a thousand thoughts simultaneously: prayers he should have said, confessions he should have heard, a young girl with blonde hair and desperate eyes who he'd failed to save. And beneath it all, a single question that his dying brain could not answer:

Why?

***

The electronic chime of his phone dragged Leland Jamo from the pleasant fog of medication-induced drowsiness. He sat in a paper exam gown on a table too narrow for comfort, his bare legs dangling like a child's, trying to remember the last time he'd felt fully rested. Days? Weeks? The timeline blurred.

He'd been forty-two for six months now, but lately he felt decades older. The face that stared back at him from bathroom mirrors had developed lines he didn't remember, gray threads in his dark hair spreading like frost across a window.

The examining room door opened. Dr. Harrison entered without knocking—a habit that had stopped bothering Jamo years ago—and set a manila folder on the counter with practiced efficiency. Mid-fifties, reading glasses perpetually perched on the end of his nose, Harrison had the resigned competence of a man who'd spent thirty years delivering mostly bad news to mostly good people.

"Your labs look fine," Harrison said, flipping through pages without making eye contact. "The only thing that comes to mind is your stressful job."

He approached Jamo and reached for his neck, fingers probing with clinical detachment. "What do you do to unwind?"

Jamo's eyes rolled up toward the stained ceiling tiles. "I really don't have much time to—"

"Mm-hmm." Harrison pressed harder beneath Jamo's jaw, checking lymph nodes or thyroid or whatever physicians checked during these ritualistic examinations. "Smoking again?"

"No." Jamo swallowed against the pressure. "I... I guess you could say I picked up an old habit."

"That right?"

"Painting."

Harrison's fingers paused for half a second before resuming their examination. "That's interesting."

"Yeah." Jamo heard the defensive edge in his own voice and tried to soften it. "Well, I've always been a good artist. Thought the painting approach would help keep things fresh. After a while it helped me see things I never caught before on the job. Details. Patterns."

Harrison stepped back and removed his hands, making notes on the folder. "Do you drink heavily?"

Jamo let out a long breath. "No."

"Any pre-existing head injuries?"

The question hit closer than Harrison probably intended. Jamo's jaw tightened. "No."

"How's your diet?"

"Junk."

"Use illegal drugs?"

Jamo gave him a look that could have frozen boiling water. Harrison had the grace to appear slightly embarrassed.

"How are your energy levels?" Harrison consulted his notes. "Do you feel tired all the time?"

"I can't remember the last time I had time to devote to sleep." The admission came out more bitter than Jamo intended. "Between cases, depositions, court appearances... I'm lucky if I get four hours."

Harrison set down his pen and met Jamo's eyes with an expression of practiced concern. "I realize that what you do seems important, and it is, but ask yourself: what is more important? Catching bad guys or being around to enjoy retirement?"

Jamo forced a smile that felt like paper stretched over broken glass.

"I don't think there's anything wrong with you physically," Harrison continued. "It could be just the normal aging process. Everyone forgets things now and then. By the sound of it, you just need a vacation."

"Can you write a prescription for that?"

Jamo slid off the table, the paper gown rustling. As his feet hit the cold floor, his phone buzzed again. He glanced at the screen and felt his stomach drop.

Captain Michaels. With the code they'd established years ago. Not urgent. Emergency.

He looked up at Harrison, who was watching him with an expression somewhere between sympathy and resignation.

"Leland," Harrison said quietly, "I've seen a lot of you guys go down this road. Being burned out at the end of a long career. Start thinking about yourself now." He paused, letting the words settle. "You can't save the world all the time."

Jamo stared at his phone. The screen's glow painted his face in cold blue light, illuminating the shadows beneath his eyes, the hollow places stress had carved into his features.

Harrison was right, of course. The job was killing him. Maybe not quickly, but steadily, like water wearing down stone. Each case took something from him—a little more sleep, a little more optimism, another fragment of the person he'd been before he started wading through humanity's worst impulses.

But the phone kept buzzing. Someone had died. Someone always died. And despite everything—the exhaustion, the memory problems, the slow dissolution of his health and sanity—Jamo knew he would answer.

Because this was what he did. This was who he was.

He'd save the world or die trying.

Even if, increasingly, he couldn't remember why.

***

The crime scene perimeter had already been established by the time Jamo arrived at Saint Anthony's. Yellow tape cordoned off the cathedral's front steps, and media vans clustered along the street like feeding vultures. Satellite dishes pointed toward gray winter sky, broadcasting towers extending upward as if trying to escape the grim business at ground level.

Jamo parked three blocks away—closer spots had been claimed by patrol cars and forensics vans—and made the walk through late afternoon cold. January in Detroit meant gray slush piled along curbs, exhaust fumes hanging in frigid air, and a penetrating dampness that found every gap in clothing. His breath created small clouds that dissipated instantly.

He'd changed into his work uniform: dark slacks, white shirt, a jacket that had seen better years. Professional but not pristine. The clothes of a man who spent his days navigating between morgues and courtrooms, never quite belonging to either world.

As he approached the police line, Captain Michaels stepped forward to meet him, checking his watch with theatrical precision.

"Don't give me that look," Jamo said, ducking under the tape. "I'm here."

Michaels—fifty-six, built like a retired linebacker, face weathered by three decades of managing crime scenes—shook his head. "It's pretty sad when the media beats the lead investigator to his own crime scene."

He gestured toward the cluster of reporters pressing against the barricades. Cameras tracked Jamo's movement, journalists shouting questions that he ignored with practiced ease.

Jamo scanned the briefing sheet a uniform had pressed into his hands.

Location: Saint Anthony's Cathedral.

Victim: Father Paul Dominic, 53.

Discovery: Custodian arriving for morning cleaning, approximately 6:45 AM.

Condition of body: See attached photographs (NOT FOR PUBLIC RELEASE).

He glanced at the photos and felt his stomach turn.

"What difference does it make?" he said, not looking up from the briefing. "Dead is dead. He's not going anywhere."

"You're going to give me a damn heart attack!" Michaels fell into step beside him as they climbed the cathedral steps. "You look like hell, by the way. When's the last time you slept?"

Jamo didn't answer. Sleep was a luxury he couldn't afford, and they both knew it.

The cathedral's interior hit him like a physical force. He'd been in countless churches over his career—crime scenes had a way of disrespecting sacred spaces—but Saint Anthony's carried a weight that went beyond architecture or history. The air itself felt heavy, oppressive, as if the building were holding its breath.

And the smell. Copper and smoke and something else. Something organic and wrong that his brain refused to process.

They walked down the center aisle, and Jamo finally looked up.

Father Paul hung upside down from the cross above the altar, his body gutted like a deer after a hunt. His cassock had been pulled up over his head, exposing the cavity where his internal organs should have been. They weren't gone—Jamo could see them arranged around the altar with disturbing precision—but their placement seemed deliberate, ritualistic.

The priest's arms had been secured to the cross's horizontal beam with what looked like his own intestines, wound around the wood and tied with grotesque care. His face, still visible beneath the bunched cassock, was frozen in an expression of absolute terror.

"What the fuck am I looking at?!" Michaels' voice cracked. In thirty years of police work, he'd seen brutality in every imaginable form. But this was different. This wasn't rage or passion or even sadism.

This was judgment.

Jamo crouched near the front pew, his mind automatically cataloging details. He pulled out his worn notebook—spiral-bound, half-filled with sketches and observations from previous cases—and began tracing an outline of the scene. His fingers moved with mechanical precision, creating a rough map of body position, blood spatter, and evidence placement.

He pulled on latex gloves, cycling his fingers in a habitual motion he didn't realize he was doing anymore. The photographer moved around him, flash bulbs popping like small explosions, each burst of light revealing new horrors.

The coroner—Dr. Lisa Chen, efficient and unflappable—worked methodically, bagging evidence with clinical detachment.

Jamo stood and moved to one of the front pews, sinking onto the hard wood. Michaels joined him, the bench creaking under their combined weight.

"Twenty-seven years," Michaels said quietly, staring at Father Paul's body. "You think you've seen it all."

Jamo pulled off the bloody gloves, careful not to touch the exterior surfaces. He'd been doing this job for eighteen years—not as long as Michaels, but long enough. Long enough to know that there was no such thing as "seeing it all." The capacity for human cruelty constantly evolved, found new depths, discovered fresh ways to shock and devastate.

"I don't know why you're still here," Jamo said. "I would have retired by now."

Michaels stretched his arms across the pew back, a gesture that might have looked relaxed if not for the rigid tension in his shoulders. "And do what?"

"Probably become an alcoholic."

"That's reassuring." Michaels attempted a smile that didn't reach his eyes. "I figure three more years will get me up to seventy-five percent of my retirement. I can cash out now with sixty-six."

Jamo ran his fingers along the pew and stopped. His thumb caught on something irregular in the wood. He looked down.

A burn mark.

Not large—maybe three inches across—but deep. The wood had been scorched to charcoal, the grain blackened and warped. He pressed his finger into it, feeling how the heat had actually altered the density of the wood, creating a depression that went a quarter-inch deep.

"Besides," Michaels continued, oblivious to Jamo's discovery, "latest statistics on retired cops say they only have a few years once they leave the job."

"Oh yeah?" Jamo's attention was fixed on the burn mark. "Then what?"

"Then we see how accurate these statistics are."

The photographer approached, camera hanging from a strap around his neck. Young guy—couldn't be more than twenty-five—with the unsettled look of someone encountering real horror for the first time.

"Detective," he said, his voice carefully controlled. "If you don't mind me asking... what could do that to the front door?"

"Do what?"

The photographer gestured toward the entrance. "The handles. They're... gone. Just holes where they should be. And the metal around the holes is all warped. Melted."

Jamo stood slowly, his knees protesting the movement. He walked back down the aisle toward the cathedral entrance, Michaels following.

The doors stood closed now, secured by crime scene investigators. But even from ten feet away, Jamo could see what the photographer meant.

Where solid brass handles had been mounted—probably since the church's construction in the 1940s—there were only holes. The edges of the metal showed clear signs of liquification. Brass had run down the wood like candle wax, solidifying in frozen drips and rivulets.

Jamo crouched, studying the damage without touching it. Brass melted at approximately 1,700 degrees Fahrenheit. To achieve that temperature required specialized equipment—industrial torches, furnaces, focused thermite reactions. Not something you carry around in your pocket.

And yet someone—something—had melted through these locks as easily as a child punching through wet paper.

"Detective Jamo?"

He turned. Dr. Chen stood near the altar, her latex gloves stained dark with blood, holding an evidence bag containing what looked like photographs.

"You need to see this," she said.

Jamo made his way back up the aisle, each step feeling heavier than the last. The photographs in Chen's evidence bag showed the same young woman repeatedly. Blonde, beautiful despite obvious drug use, captured in various states of distress and desperation.

"Found scattered around the body," Chen explained. "Arranged like some kind of trail. Leading from the doors to the altar."

Jamo took the bag, studying the images through the plastic. The girl couldn't be more than twenty. In some photos she looked directly at the camera with eyes that held equal parts fear and defiance. In others, she seemed unaware of being photographed at all, lost in whatever private hell addiction had created.

"You recognize her?" Michaels asked.

Jamo didn't answer immediately. Something about the girl's face tugged at his memory—not from his own experience, but from somewhere else. A news story perhaps. Or a missing persons bulletin.

"Run her through the database," he said finally, handing the evidence bag back to Chen. "Cross-reference with recent missing persons, drug arrests, hospital admissions."

"Already on it," Chen said.

Jamo looked back at Father Paul's body, then at the photographs, then at the melted door handles.

The pieces didn't fit together. Not yet. But they would. They always did, eventually.

Because crimes, no matter how bizarre or brutal, followed patterns. Human behavior—even at its most depraved—operated according to internal logic. Find the logic, find the perpetrator.

But as Jamo stood in the violated sanctuary of Saint Anthony's Cathedral, surrounded by evidence of violence that transcended normal human capacity, a small voice in the back of his mind whispered something he didn't want to acknowledge:

What if this wasn't human?

What if the rules he'd spent eighteen years learning no longer applied?

He pushed the thought away and focused on the physical evidence. The burn marks. The photographs. The methodical arrangement of body parts. Someone had done this. Someone with motivation, means, and opportunity.

His job was to find them.

Even if, increasingly, he wasn't sure he wanted to know what he might find.

"Detective?" Michaels' voice pulled him from his thoughts. "You okay?"

Jamo realized he'd been standing motionless, staring at the altar without seeing it. How long had he been lost in thought? Seconds? Minutes?

The memory problems Harrison had mentioned. They were getting worse.

"Yeah," he lied. "I'm fine. Just... taking it all in."

Michaels didn't look convinced, but he didn't push. One of the small mercies of a long professional relationship—knowing when to let things go.

"What do you want to do?" Michaels asked.

Jamo pulled out his notebook and turned to a fresh page. He began sketching the scene again, this time focusing on the spatial relationships. Doors. Aisle. Pews. Altar. Body.

"We need to canvass the neighborhood," he said, his pencil moving across paper in quick, confident strokes. "Someone must have seen or heard something. Church this size doesn't get violated without witnesses."

"Already started. Uniforms are going door to door."

"Good." Jamo added details to his sketch—the burn marks, the photographic trail, the position of Father Paul's remains. The act of drawing helped him think, helped him see patterns his conscious mind might miss. "What about surveillance cameras?"

"None inside the church. And the exterior cameras..." Michaels paused. "They're fried. All of them. Completely melted."

Jamo's pencil stopped moving. "Melted."

"Yeah. Like someone hit them with a blowtorch. Same as the door handles."

"Show me."

They walked outside into the gathering dusk. The temperature had dropped further, and Jamo's breath created clouds that hung in the still air. Media personnel had multiplied—apparently word had spread about the spectacular nature of the crime. Cameras tracked their movement as Michaels led him to the side of the building.

The security camera hung from its mount like a Salvador Dalí painting. The plastic housing had partially liquified, creating grotesque drips and whorls. The lens had cracked from thermal stress, and the metal mounting bracket showed signs of extreme heat exposure.

"There are three more just like it," Michaels said. "Every camera covering the cathedral entrances. Whoever did this knew exactly where to look."

Jamo examined the damaged camera without touching it. The precision bothered him. This wasn't random vandalism or opportunistic destruction. Someone had systematically eliminated every potential source of evidence.

"Or they don't care if we see them," he said quietly.

"What?"

"Nothing." Jamo stepped back. "Let's get forensics to document all of this. Heat signatures, metal analysis, everything."

"Already called them."

"Good."

They stood in silence for a moment, watching the last daylight fade from the sky. Streetlights flickered on along the block, creating pools of sodium-yellow illumination that somehow made the darkness between them seem deeper.

"Leland," Michaels said, using Jamo's first name—something he rarely did. "What are we dealing with here?"

It was the question Jamo had been avoiding. The question he didn't want to answer because he didn't have an answer. Not one that made sense. Not one that fit into his carefully constructed understanding of how the world worked.

"I don't know," he admitted. "But I'm going to find out."

Michaels nodded, accepting this non-answer with the resignation of someone who'd learned not to expect certainty in an uncertain world.

They walked back inside. Dr. Chen had finished her preliminary examination and was directing her team in the collection of biological evidence. The photographer continued documenting every angle, every detail, building a visual archive of horror.

Jamo returned to the pew with the burn mark and sat down. He pulled out his notebook and opened to a fresh page.

At the top, he wrote: Saint Anthony's Cathedral - Father Paul Dominic.

Below that, he began listing everything he knew for certain:

1. Victim: Catholic priest, 53, no known enemies

2. Method: Evisceration (postmortem?)

3. Evidence: Photographs of unknown female

4. Physical anomalies: Extreme heat damage (door handles, cameras, pew)

5. Timing: Overnight (between 10 PM and 6 AM)

6. Witnesses: None identified

7. Surveillance: Destroyed

He stared at the list. Seven facts. Seven pieces of a puzzle that refused to form a coherent picture.

His pencil moved to the bottom of the page, almost of its own accord, and drew a question mark.

Then, beside it, he sketched something he'd been trying not to think about. The burn pattern on the pew. The precise shape of it.

It looked like a handprint.

A very large handprint.

With fingers that ended in claws.

Jamo closed the notebook and stood. His body ached—knees, back, shoulders. The accumulated damage of eighteen years spent hunched over crime scenes, sitting in unmarked cars, chasing suspects through urban decay, poor diet and lack of exercise.

Harrison's words echoed in his mind: You can't save the world all the time.

But Father Paul had deserved saving. Had deserved protection. Had deserved better than to die terrified and alone in his own church, gutted like an animal and displayed like a warning.

A warning to whom? About what?

Jamo didn't know.

Not yet.

But he would find out. He would follow the evidence wherever it led, no matter how strange or terrible the destination might be.

Because this was what he did. This was who he was.

Even if he couldn't remember why anymore.

Even if the price might be higher than he could afford to pay.

The cathedral's shadows lengthened as night claimed the building. Votive candles had been extinguished by crime scene technicians, leaving only harsh fluorescent work lights that created stark contrasts between light and darkness.

In those shadows, Jamo thought he saw something move.

Just for a second. Just at the edge of perception.

A shape that was too large to be human.

Eyes that burned with golden light.

He blinked, and it was gone.

Stress, he told himself. Exhaustion. The power of suggestion working on an overtired mind.

But his hand moved to his service weapon anyway, fingers brushing the grip with practiced ease.

Just in case.

Just in case the impossible had become possible.

Just in case the world had rules he didn't understand yet.

In the darkness at the back of Saint Anthony's Cathedral, something watched.

And waited.

And remembered a priest who had tried to protect a girl he had no chance of saving.

The investigation had begun.

Jamo didn't realize yet that he wasn't hunting a killer.

He was being hunted himself.

By something that had been hunting for one hundred years.

And never, ever missed its prey.

Chapter 2
FIERY EYES

The photographs haunted Jamo throughout the night.

He'd left them at the precinct—evidence didn't come home, that was protocol—but their images followed him anyway, burned into his mind with the same precision they'd been burned into Father Paul's organs. A young woman with blonde hair. Scared eyes. Track marks on her arms like a roadmap of poor decisions.

Someone's daughter. Someone's failure.

The thought wouldn't leave him alone as he navigated Detroit's late-night traffic, streetlights painting his windshield in rhythmic bursts of sodium yellow. The city looked different at this hour—more honest, maybe. The pretense of daylight commerce stripped away, leaving only what Detroit had become. Abandoned storefronts with plywood windows. Strip clubs advertising "GIRLS GIRLS GIRLS" in desperate neon. Liquor stores with bars on the windows and despair in the doorways.

Jamo had lived here his entire life. Watched the city's slow collapse like watching a loved one die by inches. Sometimes he wondered if he was dying with it.

His parking garage greeted him with familiar mechanical indifference. The door shuddered upward, protesting each inch of movement. Jamo didn't wait for it to reach full height before pulling in—three more inches of clearance than he needed, same as always. Routine meant efficiency. Efficiency meant survival.

He navigated to his numbered space and killed the engine. Reached for the Ho-Ho he'd been saving—his one concession to dinner—and found only an empty wrapper.

"Shit."

The wrapper crinkled accusingly in his hand. When had he eaten it? This morning? Yesterday? The memory refused to surface, another casualty of his deteriorating recall.

He moved to open his door and stopped. The car next to his—a battered Toyota with a "COEXIST" bumper sticker and two flat tires—was parked directly on the yellow line. Too close. Way too close.

Jamo pressed his face against the window, confirming what he already knew. Maybe six inches of clearance. Not enough to squeeze through, not without dislocating something.

"Son-of-a... fuckin'... Jesus!"

He slammed his palm against the steering wheel, then immediately felt ridiculous for the outburst. The car didn't care. The absent Toyota owner didn't care. The universe, as usual, didn't care.

Jamo swept the accumulated wrappers from his passenger seat to the floor—adding to the archaeological layers of junk food packaging that documented his dietary decline—and climbed over the center console. His knee caught the gear shift. His elbow hit the window button, creating a pneumatic wheeze as the glass lowered six inches before he could stop it.

By the time he emerged from the passenger door, his dignity felt as battered as the Toyota.

The building's lobby smelled like industrial cleaner and old carpet. Jamo's mailbox yielded the usual haul: bills he couldn't quite afford, advertisements for things he'd never buy, and a credit card offer promising to solve problems it would only worsen.

He pressed the elevator button and waited, watching the numbers descend with glacial patience. Four. Three. Two.

The doors opened to reveal Mrs. Dowling—eighty something, cane in one hand, a dust-mop dog in the other.

The creature looked at Jamo and growled, a sound more wheeze than threat.

"Oh! Heavens, thank you, Leland." Mrs. Dowling shuffled forward, moving with the cautious precision of someone whose bones had turned to porcelain.

"How are you, Mrs. Dowling?" Jamo held the elevator door, feeling it try to close against his hand every three seconds. A mechanical reminder that patience had limits.

"You working late tonight, I see?"

"Just coming in off my shift."

The elevator door bounced against his hand again. Mrs. Dowling continued her exit with all the urgency of continental drift.

"Every time I see you, Leland, you're coming home from work."

"Seems that way, huh?" Jamo forced a smile. "Guess I work a lot these days."

"Doesn't leave much time to spend with that nice girl I see you with... Beth, is it?"

The name landed like a punch to somewhere soft and vital. Beth. Four months since she'd walked out, taking her toothbrush and her patience and any illusion that Jamo's job hadn't consumed everything worth having.

"Oh, Mrs. Dowling, I haven't seen Beth for almost four months now."

The elevator door clicked again, more insistently.

"See? That's because you work too much." Mrs. Dowling poked him with her cane, a gesture that somehow combined affection and accusation. "You'll never find yourself getting married that way, Leland."

The dog growled again. Jamo wondered if it was trained to emphasize her points.

"Right about that one, Mrs. Dowling."

She turned and began her journey toward the lobby doors. "Of course I am. My Frank, god rest his soul, always said you were his best officer."

Frank Dowling. Dead three years now. Heart attack at his desk, pen still in hand. The good ones always went that way—still trying to serve even as their bodies quit.

"He was a good man," Jamo said.

"He also said that you work too hard."

"I guess you're both right."

The dog looked back over Mrs. Dowling's shoulder, its bulging eyes fixing on Jamo with what might have been judgment or digestive distress. Jamo made a throat-cutting gesture at it.

The dog growled.

Jamo turned back to the elevator, but the doors had already closed. He sighed and pressed the button again.

Some days, even the machinery was against you.

His apartment greeted him with the silence of neglect. Jamo flicked the light switch and surveyed his kingdom—a bachelor's accommodation that had somehow failed to graduate past college aesthetics despite his forty-two years. Simple furniture that came from stores with names like "ValueHome" and "FurniturePlex." A couch he'd owned for eight years. A TV that only got basic cable.

On the wall beside the door hung framed newspaper clippings documenting a younger Jamo receiving commendations, shaking hands with commissioners and mayors. One showed him in uniform, his hair darker, his face unmarked by the slow erosion of optimism. The headline read: "Officer burned trying to save girl."

He didn't look at that one anymore.

In the kitchen, his nightly routine unfolded with practiced efficiency. Keys in the bowl. Change in the bowl. Receipts crumpled and tossed toward the trash can—two points, nothing but rim. The "#1 Son" mug still sat in the sink, a Mother's Day gift from years ago that he couldn't bring himself to put in the cupboard. Something about leaving it out felt like keeping her company.

He opened the refrigerator. Fruit and vegetables his mother had forced on him during their last lunch occupied the crisper drawer with the resignation of condemned prisoners. Behind them, safely shielded from accidental health, sat a six-pack of beer.

Jamo grabbed one and kicked the refrigerator door closed.

In the living room, he hung his jacket and pressed play on his answering machine, collapsing onto the couch with a grunt that sounded older than he felt.

"Leland here. I'm never home, so leave me a message or call my cell which I probably won't answer anyway... BEEP!"

His mother's voice filled the apartment: "Leland, it's your mother. You've probably already left for work. I just wanted to say thank you for lunch yesterday. It was great to see you. You look so tired all the time though. What did the doctor have to say about your memory?"

Jamo flipped through his mail. Bills. Junk. A letter from the City of Detroit's Department of Legal Affairs with the ominous weight of official consequences.

His mother continued: "Have you been eating the fruit I gave you? Fruit is food for thought. The avocados are delicious, I made guacamole with mine, oh... I should have given you—BEEP!"

The machine cut her off mid-thought. Jamo opened the legal letter and felt his stomach sink.

Notice of disposition regarding the lawsuit filed for damages resulting from the child lost in the fire. Case number. Court date. Liability determination pending.

The little girl's face flashed through his mind—eyes wide with terror, smoke billowing, flames that moved with hungry intelligence. His hands had reached for her. The floor had given way. She'd fallen into fire that consumed her in seconds while he'd clung to burning timber, his left side blistering and cracking like meat on a grill.

He'd saved no one that day.

The answering machine beeped again: "This is Judith from the city library, calling Mr. Leland Jamo as a reminder regarding overdue books: Theoretical Physics and Our Universe, Clinical Depression: A Light in the Dark, and The World of Pastries. Please return them as soon as possible. Thank you. BEEP!"

Jamo raised his middle finger to the machine and took a long pull of beer.

The spare room called to him the way it always did. Not quite an office, not quite a studio. A liminal space where Jamo kept the parts of himself that didn't fit the detective mold.

He flicked the light on and took in his sanctuary. An old desk salvaged from a yard sale. A wooden office chair from the 1920s with a cracked leather seat that conformed to his body like a worn glove. And paintings. Dozens of them, in various stages of completion, leaning against walls or stacked in corners.

Crime scenes. All of them. Rendered in oils with photographic precision.

The church where Mrs. Chen had been found strangled. The warehouse where the Martinez brothers had executed three rivals. The pawnshop that had become a tomb for its owner. Each painting captured details his conscious mind had processed but not fully registered—patterns in blood spatter, the precise angle of a body's fall, the way light fell through windows at the moment of death.

Painting helped him see. Helped him remember. Helped him solve cases that his exhausted detective's brain might otherwise miss.

He set up a fresh canvas on the easel by the window and began mixing colors on his palette. The CD player came to life at his touch—Miles Davis, Kind of Blue—and Jamo lost himself in the methodical act of creation.

His shirt came off, exposing the burn scars that wrapped his left torso like a topographical map of trauma. The skin there never tanned, never quite moved right. A permanent reminder of the day he'd learned that heroism and tragedy were often the same thing viewed from different angles.

He applied paint in careful strokes, building Father Paul's cathedral from memory. The Gothic arches. The altar. The way candlelight had played across stone and shadow. His brush moved almost without conscious direction, his mind elsewhere while his hands documented horror.

Outside, rain began to fall. Jamo paused to stare through the window, watching water streak the glass and distort the streetlights below. The rhythm of rain matched the rhythm of his brushstrokes. Drip. Stroke. Drip. Stroke.

Flashes invaded his concentration:

Fire. Not the cathedral.

Somewhere else. Somewhere older.

A young girl's voice screaming. Not the girl from the legal notice. Someone different. Younger. More desperate.

Jamo's hand froze mid-stroke, the brush trembling slightly. The memory—if it was a memory—evaporated like smoke, leaving only unease in its wake.

He blinked and looked at the canvas. Without realizing it, he'd painted Father Paul's church with surprising accuracy. The pews. The altar. The cross where the body had hung. Even the burn marks on the wood, rendered in blacks and deep umbers that suggested heat beyond normal comprehension.

How long had he been painting? Minutes? Hours?

The light through his window had changed. Dawn approached, turning the sky from black to deep purple. Jamo's phone vibrated on the desk, making him jump.

"This is Jamo." His voice came out rough, unused. "Be there in ten."

He hung up and stared at the painting. It was good. Too good. The kind of detailed accuracy that came from obsession or mental illness or whatever neurological quirk was slowly unraveling his memory.

The cathedral stared back at him from canvas, keeping its secrets.

***

The morgue smelled like formaldehyde and industrial cleaner with an undertone of something organic and wrong that no amount of ventilation could quite eliminate. Jamo had been visiting this building for eighteen years and had never gotten used to that smell. You didn't get used to it. You just stopped noticing it consciously while it burrowed into your clothes and hair like a spectral passenger.

Dr. Lisa Chen looked up from her examination table as Jamo pushed through the swinging doors. She was in her mid-forties, efficient and unflappable, with the kind of detached professionalism that came from spending your days elbow-deep in human remains.

"No peeking, Jamo." She moved to intercept him before he could lift the sheet covering Father Paul's remains. "I don't think you want to compromise another case."

"I wasn't—"

"Sure you weren't."

Chen grabbed the sheet and pulled it back with the casual authority of someone who owned this space. What remained of Father Paul lay exposed under harsh fluorescent light, sectioned and cataloged, reduced to components.

"I've never seen anything like this before," Chen said, gesturing to the organs arranged on a secondary table. "Maybe you can make something of it."

Each organ—heart, kidneys, liver, sections of intestine—bore burn marks. Not random scorch marks, but deliberate patterns seared into tissue with precise heat.

"Anything you come across, gang symbol maybe?" Chen asked.

Jamo leaned in, putting on his reading glasses. The marks resolved into familiar shapes. Circles. Lines. The same partial symbol he'd seen at the church. The same symbol that had appeared on Carlos Javier's neck.

"No... Nothing I've ever seen." He paused, registering what she'd said. "Wait, is that a piece of fruit?"

"That's a kidney."

"Oh." Jamo straightened, suddenly self-conscious. "Got fruit on the mind lately."

Chen gestured to the other organs, each bearing similar marks. "Typically with violent cases we would find skin tissue or blood beneath the fingernails." She lifted Father Paul's hand, turning it to catch the light. "But this guy only has his own tissue under them."

"No defensive wounds either," Jamo observed, studying the unmarred arms.

"Nothing to indicate any." Chen's voice carried a note of professional puzzlement. "He doesn't have any superficial lesions, bruises, signs of blunt trauma... kinda like he let it happen."

"Who sits down and takes something like this without any kind of fight or struggle?"

Jamo's phone buzzed: 10-49. Another body.

"Jesus!"

"Work never ends in your field," Chen said.

He showed her the code. Her expression shifted from curiosity to recognition.

"Hmmm... or mine, I see."

"So what about the lack of blood?" Jamo pocketed his phone. "How does someone dismember a live body without getting a single drop somewhere?"

"In my professional opinion?" Chen paused for effect. "It seems like someone took a hot object and used it to sear through his entire anatomy, piece by piece."

"You mean cauterized everything as he sliced him up?"

"It looks that way."

Jamo leaned closer, examining one of the cauterized wounds. The edges of the tissue were smooth, almost glassy. Whatever heat had done this had been intense enough to flash-boil blood and seal vessels simultaneously.

"So what kind of instrument can do that?"

"I couldn't say offhand..." Chen considered. "A super-heated blade? Laser?"

"Should I put out an APB on Flash Gordon?"

"I could see that he let it happen if he was dead."

"Huh?"

"All the evidence suggests that he was alive." Chen pointed to Father Paul's upper arm, where faint marks showed in the cauterized flesh. "I can only speculate of course, but I'd say he was being held up with the very object that tore into him."

She moved to another table bearing Father Paul's severed thighs. "The samples taken under his fingernails match his own DNA, which match the dig marks on his thighs, and are the only wounds that show any sign of bleeding."

Jamo followed her gesture to the neck region. "These dig marks here, however, have a larger groove than you see on his thigh. Much larger. And have the same distinct cauterizing burn mark. Much more distinct than the others. Almost like..."

"Like what?"

Chen held up her hands, positioning them over the marks. Her fingers didn't come close to matching the grooves. "Almost like the mark of a man's hands. Except hot enough to burn into him."

Jamo's phone buzzed again—an update on the call.

"Detective, this is a premature meeting. Go to your call. I'll have a full report for you and hopefully know more."

"Yeah. Okay." Jamo backed toward the exit, still staring at the marks. "You call me as soon as you find anything."

Handprints.

Someone—something—with hands large enough and hot enough to burn through flesh had held Father Paul while taking him apart.

Jamo pushed through the morgue doors into gray morning light, trying to reconcile what he'd seen with anything that made sense in a world governed by physical laws.

He failed.

The alleyway looked different in daylight. Less menacing, maybe, but more pathetic. The bricks were tagged with spray-painted declarations of territory and desire. Trash piled against dumpsters like urban sediment. A used condom lay in a puddle, surrounded by cigarette butts and broken glass—the detritus of desperation.

Blue lights flashed against wet brick. Officers moved through the scene with practiced efficiency, creating a perimeter, documenting evidence, doing the careful dance of preservation before lawyers and judges got involved.

Jamo handed his card to the photographer. "Get me copies."

The kid—and he was a kid, couldn't be more than twenty-five—recognized him immediately.

"Sure, Detective."

"Three-in-ones and close-ups of anything... strange."

The photographer gave him a look that said, "Don't tell me how to do my job," but nodded anyway.

Jamo approached a cluster of uniforms. "Someone want to give me the low down?"

A young officer with a name tag reading "MARTINEZ" stepped forward. "We got dispatched with Rescue to a man-down call. First on scene, I walk in, see a decapitated body."

He pointed toward a dumpster twenty feet away. "Where's the head?"

"About three feet from the body, sir."

"There's also a woman's jacket lying near the body. That's all I saw before I traced my steps back and sealed the area off."

Jamo surveyed the crime scene with new eyes. Martinez had done it right—preserved the evidence, minimized contamination. "Good job. Any witnesses?"

"911 call was anonymous. Sarge has a crew canvasing and questioning the neighborhood, but right now we got jack to go on."

"Okay. Keep me informed."

Jamo moved toward the dumpster, pulling on latex gloves and cycling his fingers in that unconscious habit he couldn't quite break. The body lay sprawled beside the dumpster, headless, cauterized at the neck. No blood. Just like Father Paul. Just like everything about this case that made no goddamn sense.

He knelt beside the corpse, examining the neck wound. The edges showed the same glassy smoothness—heat intense enough to seal tissue instantly. Around the wound, the skin bore scorch marks in patterns that looked almost deliberate.

"No blood," he muttered, moving to examine the severed head.

It had rolled against the brick wall, coming to rest face-up. The eyes were still open, frozen in an expression somewhere between shock and terror. The base of the neck showed the same cauterization, the same impossible precision.

Jamo looked back toward the photographer. "Hey! You got all this?"

"Yep."

A leather jacket lay crumpled near the body, sleeves showing distinct scorch marks. Jamo lifted it carefully, noting the pattern. The burns matched the placement on Father Paul's arms. And there—on the sleeve itself—the same partial symbol. Seared into the leather like a brand.

"I hope you're not stealing my evidence."

Jamo turned to find Brecken standing behind him, coffee in hand, looking remarkably well-rested for someone investigating multiple homicides. Randy Brecken was everything Jamo wasn't—organized, balanced, capable of maintaining relationships outside of work. Goatee always trimmed. Salt-and-pepper hair always styled. The kind of cop who went home at the end of shift and actually had something to go home to.

"Not likely." Jamo stood, holding up the evidence bag containing white powder he'd found in the jacket pocket. He extended his gloved hand for a shake.

Brecken raised an eyebrow at the latex and left him hanging. Jamo converted the gesture into a middle finger and smiled.

"I thought you were on another camping trip or something."

"I do have a life outside police work, Jamo."

Jamo ignored the comment—having this conversation again felt pointless—and moved back to the severed head. "Look familiar?"

Brecken sipped his coffee, the steam rising in the cold air. "Carlos Javier. Small-time meth pusher."

"Was a small-time meth pusher." Jamo knelt again, examining the neck wound from a new angle. "The dumbass that almost blew himself up creating a lab in his basement... And I actually remember that."

The fact that he remembered felt worth noting. Small victories in the war against his deteriorating recall.

Brecken moved forward, pulling on gloves. "No big loss. What's this?"

He knelt beside what looked like a knife handle lying in a puddle. The blade was gone—melted into a twisted stub of metal that dripped toward the ground like frozen tears.

"Looks like a knife handle... look at the blade."

They both examined it, Brecken rotating the remains in the light. The metal had liquified, then resolidified in mid-drip. Whatever heat had done this exceeded anything Jamo had encountered in eighteen years of investigating Detroit's worst.

"It's melted off. What the hell could do that?"

"Buck Rogers, maybe?"

"What?"

Jamo shrugged and turned his attention to the body. The partial symbol on Carlos's neck caught his eye. He'd seen it before. At the church. On Father Paul's organs. On this jacket. The pattern was repeating with disturbing consistency.

"This guy looks like he was probed with a cattle iron," Brecken observed. "Where's all the blood?"

"There isn't any."

"All this and no blood?"

"Same M.O. as the Father Paul scene."

Brecken gave him a confused look. Right—he'd been on that camping trip when they'd found the priest. Missing pieces of shared knowledge meant wasted time explaining.

"Oh, right, you weren't there."

Jamo grabbed Carlos's head and—before Brecken could object—placed it back on the body. The move was macabre but necessary. When the head connected to the neck, the partial symbols aligned, creating a complete mark.

"I've seen that a few times today," Jamo said, studying the completed symbol.

"Seen what?"

"That symbol. It was all over the priest's body, that jacket... This guy's neck."

He motioned the photographer over and made a quick sketch in his notebook. The symbol resolved into clear lines—a circle bisected by a cross, flames curling around it like serpents.

The camera flash popped, freezing the moment in chemical silver.

Jamo stared at his sketch. The symbol meant something. Had significance beyond mere decoration. Somewhere in Detroit's archives or online databases or locked in someone's memory, this mark had meaning.

He just had to find it.

The police precinct hummed with afternoon energy—phones ringing, computers clicking, the low murmur of dozens of conversations blending into white noise. Jamo sat at his desk in the detective bureau, clicking through gang symbol databases with the methodical determination of someone who knew the answer existed but couldn't quite find it.

Across from him, Brecken typed up reports with the efficient speed of someone who'd done this ten thousand times before.

"Why is it that I always end up doing all the paperwork?" Brecken asked without looking up from his keyboard.

"You always get to it first."

"That's not true. You just never take the initiative."

"That is true, but..." Jamo paused, his train of thought derailing. What had he been about to say? The words had been right there, and now they were gone, evaporated like morning mist. He went back to reading the screen.

"But what?"

"But... uhhh... you're the better writer. I've... uh, always said you should be a writer."

"You've never said that before."

Jamo stared at his monitor, watching the cursor blink in the search box. Flash. Flash. Flash. Hypnotic.

Time seemed to stretch and compress simultaneously. How long had he been staring?

"Jamo..."

No response. The cursor kept blinking.

"Jamo! You really think I should be a writer?"

Jamo snapped back to awareness and began typing, trying to cover the lapse. "What? Yeah, sure. That symbol..."

He pointed at the screen where he'd managed to navigate to a Catholic imagery database. The search had happened without his conscious direction, his detective's instinct working while his mind wandered.

Brecken stood and walked over, coffee mug in hand.

"The mark I keep finding at these crime scenes..." Jamo clicked through pages of religious symbolism. "I first saw it at the church where the priest was found and then it shows up burned onto his body. Then in that alleyway on Javier and that woman's jacket..."

"The thing that looked like a cross?"

Jamo found it—the symbol from his sketch, rendered in medieval woodcut style on a page about fallen angels. Next to it, an artist's rendering of a hulking figure wreathed in flames, standing within a circle of arcane glyphs.

"It's the symbol of a fallen angel."

"A fallen angel?"

The description scrolled across the screen in archaic language:

Flauros, the Sixty-Fourth Spirit. A Great Duke who appeareth as a mighty, terrible and strong human shape with eyes flaming and fiery with most terrible countenance. He giveth true answers of all things, Present, Past, and to Come. He destroyeth and burneth up those who be the Enemies of the Exorcist, should he so desire it. He is constrained by divine virtue to burn and destroy all the conjurer's adversaries.*

"Says it's the symbol of Flauros, a fallen angel," Jamo read aloud. "According to the Dead Sea Scrolls, it means the 'Sons of God' or the 'Descendants of Seth.' Flauros is one of these 'Sons of God' cast out of heaven along with one third of the angels. They fell for nine days, sometime around the 15th century."

Brecken leaned in, reading over his shoulder. "Think these murders are part of some subversive Catholic cult?"

"Not exactly." Jamo removed his gun from his hip—the holster was digging into his side—and got more comfortable. "He's some sort of demon, according to this. Flauros is the sixty-fourth spirit. 'At the command of thirty legions, he is a Great Duke and appeareth as a mighty, terrible and strong human shape with eyes flaming and fiery with most terrible countenance. He giveth true answers of all things, Present, Past, and to Come. He destroyeth and burneth up those who be the Enemies of the Exorcist, should he so desire it. He is constrained by divine virtue to burn and destroy all the conjurer's adversaries.'"

"We needeth to find out if there are any cults that worship this guy," Brecken said in mock-medieval tones.

Both their phones beeped simultaneously.

"I got it." Brecken grabbed his desk phone and dialed. "Detective Brecken... yeah, we're working that one. Seventh and Main? What time? Where is she now?"

He started scribbling notes. Jamo kept typing, searching for cult references, finding mostly conspiracy theories and role-playing game forums.

"When did they send her over? Thanks." Brecken hung up. "That was the desk Sergeant downstairs. Said a distraught girl came in last night claiming she was in that alleyway over on Main when Javier lost his head."

Jamo spun his chair around.

"We're just getting this now?!"

"He was approving reports and caught it, spoke to the guys. They thought she was just a crazy woman."

"A crazy witness."

"She claims something saved her."

Jamo stood, energized by the first real lead they'd had all day. "Where is she now?"

"Henry Ford Hospital."

"Henry Ford?"

"She was sent for psych evaluation."

"That was fast. We didn't even get a chance to question her."

Jamo's pager vibrated: Michaels.

"Shit. It's Michaels."

Both men left to his office with anticipation of what they felt would be an unnecessary ass chewing.

Captain Michaels stood with his back to them, staring out the window of his office with the posture of a man who'd been given orders he despised but had no choice but to follow. His coffee sat untouched on the desk, steam long since dissipated.

Jamo and Brecken found their seats and waited.

"I'm guessing you two have already heard about the crazy girl that came in last night."

"Uh... yeah, we just got that call. We were—"

"No you're not."

Jamo sat forward. "But we—"

Michaels turned, his face set in the rigid mask of bureaucratic resignation. "She's off limits."

"We haven't interviewed her yet. How are we—"

"I'm sorry, my hands are tied, which means, so are yours." Michaels moved to his desk but didn't sit. "About twenty minutes ago there were a bunch of bureaucrats in here giving me a bunch of BS about due process and unfortunate circumstantial happenstance. I don't even know if I understand everything they said. All I know is that they want her left alone."

Brecken tried a different angle. "What about the video or recordings from her statement?"

"Confiscated until further notice."

"Well, how are we supposed to investigate a murder and protect these fair streets if our only witness is off limits... sir?"

The pause before "sir" carried more weight than the word itself.

"The best way you can under the circumstances..." Michaels finally sat, the chair groaning under his weight. "Look, I'm as frustrated as you are, Detective, but this is how things trickle downhill and now I'm asking you and Randy to get out there and find me a perpetrator. The girl mentioned to the guys downstairs that there were two assailants in that alley. Go find out who the other one was... and don't bother that girl."

Jamo opened his mouth to argue, saw the futility in Michaels' expression, and closed it again.

They left the office without slamming the door, though Jamo wanted to.The parking structure echoed with their footsteps as Jamo and Brecken made their way to the car.

"So what makes this girl so important that the police aren't even allowed to talk to her?" Jamo asked.

"Maybe she's connected to someone politically... endowed?"

"Okay. Good theory. Then why wouldn't this someone want us to talk to her?"

"Because of what she knows?"

"And she knows who killed Javier and possibly Father Paul..."

They reached the car. Jamo unlocked it, and they slid into their respective seats. Brecken shuffled his feet through the accumulated wrappers on the floorboard, trying to find stable ground. "So what does that mean?"

Jamo started the engine. "We ask her."

"Just because you don't like your job doesn't mean I don't."

Jamo backed out of the space without answering. Some decisions didn't require discussion.

They were going to the hospital.

Orders or no orders.

Henry Ford Hospital's psychiatric ward occupied the fourth floor, accessible only by special elevator codes and staff credentials. The walls were painted in what some consultant probably called "soothing neutrals"—beiges and soft grays designed to calm agitated minds. Jamo thought they looked like the color of surrender.

Dr. Hinkley met them outside Exam Room 7, his expression a mix of professional concern and administrative anxiety.

"Who are you?"

"I'm Detective Brecken and this is my partner Detective Jamo. We need to speak with Ms. Harris, if possible."

They showed their badges. Hinkley's jaw tightened.

"You guys know the deal. She's under psychiatric care. She's not in a state to be interviewed. You know that anything she says would be suppressed by the courts."

"Yeah, we know the fruit from the poison tree routine, okay." Jamo stepped closer, using his height advantage. "We just need to get a little information out of her about a homicide."

"If we don't, this case may go cold," Brecken added, playing good cop to Jamo's impatience.

Hinkley looked between them, calculating the political ramifications of cooperation versus obstruction.

"Gentlemen, this is a very sensitive predicament. We could all be fired with one phone call to her people..."

"Family?"

"You know I can't tell you that."

"Listen, a priest was murdered." Jamo's voice dropped to something hard and final. "Report it if you have to. We need some leads."

Hinkley considered, then gave in with the resignation of someone who'd learned that rules and reality rarely aligned. "Do what you got to do. She's been mildly sedated. Just don't give her a hard time. She seemed pretty shaken up."

He stepped aside, granting access.

The exam room was standard medical—sterile surfaces, monitoring equipment, the smell of antiseptic and fear. Christy Harris sat on the bed, her blonde hair tangled, her eyes glazed with whatever they'd given her to calm down. But even sedated, even worn by addiction and trauma, she possessed an ethereal quality that made Jamo understand why someone would photograph her obsessively.

She looked up as they entered, and Jamo saw it—the same face from the photographs at Father Paul's church. The same frightened eyes.

"Ms. Harris?" Brecken's voice was gentle, almost fatherly. "I'm Detective Brecken. This is Detective Jamo.

We'd like to ask you a few questions about what happened last night."

Christy's gaze focused on them with effort. "You won't believe me."

"Try us," Jamo said.

She laughed—a sound somewhere between humor and hysteria. "Nobody ever believes me. That's why I'm here. That's why they always send me here."

"What happened in that alley, Christy?"

Her eyes went distant, seeing something beyond the hospital walls. "He saved me. The thing with the fiery eyes. He saved me."

"Who saved you?"

"I don't know what he is." Her voice dropped to a whisper. "But he looked into me. Really looked into me. Like he could see... everything. And then Carlos was gone and Freddy was running and I was on the ground and my jacket was smoking and—"

She stopped, her breath coming faster. The heart monitor beside the bed picked up the rhythm, translating fear into electronic beeps.

"It's okay," Brecken said. "Take your time."

"His eyes..." Christy looked directly at Jamo. "They burned. Like looking into the sun, but golden. And when he touched me, my jacket started burning. Not like fire.

Like... like heat from inside him. Coming through his hands."

Jamo pulled out his notebook and the sketch of the symbol. "Did you see this mark anywhere?"

Christy stared at the drawing. Her pupils dilated despite the sedatives. "On Carlos. On the... the thing's robes. Everywhere. It was burning everywhere."

"The thing's robes?"

"The one with the fiery eyes. He wore something dark. Like a cloak or... I don't know. It didn't move right. Like the fabric was afraid of him too."

Brecken and Jamo exchanged glances.

"Christy," Jamo said carefully, "do you know why this thing would save you? Have you seen it before?"

"Sometimes." Her voice grew quieter. "Sometimes I think I see it watching. On rooftops. In alleys. Places I shouldn't go but I go anyway because..." She trailed off.

"Because why?"

"Because I can't stop." Tears ran down her face, cutting tracks through makeup and grime. "I can't stop and Father Paul tried to help me and my mother hates me and now Father Paul is dead and it's all my fault—"

"Whoa, slow down." Jamo crouched beside the bed, bringing himself to her eye level.

"What about Father Paul?"

"She killed him." Christy's voice was barely audible. "My mother. She killed him because he was trying to protect me. Just like she kills everything that tries to help me."

"Your mother?" Brecken had his notepad out now. "Who's your mother, Christy?"

"You know who she is." Christy laughed again, that broken sound. "Everyone knows who she is. That's why they won't let you talk to me. That's why I'm always protected and always alone and always—"

Dr. Hinkley burst through the door. "That's enough. Her vitals are spiking. You need to leave. Now."

"Just one more—"

"Now!"

Jamo stood slowly, holding Christy's gaze. "We're going to figure this out. I promise."

She smiled sadly. "Nobody ever figures it out, Detective. That's the point."

In the hallway, Brecken grabbed Jamo's arm. "Run her name. Full background check. I want to know who this mother is and why she's got enough pull to lock us out of our own investigation."

"Already on it."

They were halfway to the elevator when Jamo's phone rang.

"Jamo... What? When?... Jesus Christ. We're on our way."

He hung up and looked at Brecken. "They found another body. Abandoned train yard on the East Side."

"Same M.O.?"

"No." Jamo's expression was grim. "This time there's a witness. A kid. Says he saw the thing with fiery eyes."

The elevator doors opened. They stepped inside.

"He describe it?" Brecken asked.

"Yeah." Jamo pressed the button for ground floor. "Looked into me," he said. "Just like Christy."

The doors closed on their reflection—two detectives chasing something that shouldn't exist, hunting a killer that might not be human, trying to solve a case that defied every rule they'd learned.

Outside, the sun was setting.

Night was coming.

And somewhere in Detroit's abandoned places, something with golden eyes was watching.

Waiting.

Remembering a woman named Marybeth who had looked just like Christy Harris.

And burning with a rage that had smoldered for one hundred years.

CHAPTER 3
THE GIRL IN THE PHOTOS

The sedation pulled Christy Harris under like dark water closing over her head. One moment she was trying to explain about the fiery eyes, about Carlos and the thing that had saved her, and the next moment the world dissolved into pharmaceutical fog. Her last conscious thought was that the detective looked sad. Tired and sad, like someone who'd been carrying heavy things for too long.

Dr. Hinkley stood outside Exam Room 7, cell phone pressed to his ear, his voice low but urgent. Jamo watched from twenty feet away, noting the body language—hunched shoulders, furtive glances, the way the doctor turned his back to the hallway. Calling someone who didn't want to be disturbed. Someone with enough power to make a doctor nervous.

"We don't have much time," Jamo said to Brecken. "Doc is probably dialing the station now. Or someone higher up the food chain."

Brecken studied Christy through the window. She'd settled into sleep, her face relaxed for the first time since they'd seen her. Without the fear and chemical need, she looked impossibly young. "You think she's any relation to Senator Harris?"

"I'm thinking, yeah."

"Explains all the red tape."

The name had been nagging at Jamo since he'd first seen the photographs at Saint Anthony's. Harris wasn't exactly an uncommon name, but the way Michaels had shut them down, the bureaucratic intervention, the sealed witness statements—all of it pointed to someone with serious political juice. And Senator Elizabeth Harris was nothing if not juice. Two terms in the state senate, rumored gubernatorial ambitions, and enough connections to make careers or destroy them with a phone call.

If Christy was her daughter, no wonder they were being cock-blocked at every turn.

"Listen," Jamo said, making a decision. "You go talk to that kid in Room Four and see what he's got to say. I'll meet you out front."

Brecken nodded and headed down the hall. Jamo returned to Christy's room, moving quietly despite his size. She lay curled on her side, hospital gown twisted around her thin frame, blonde hair splayed across the pillow like spilled light.

"Ms. Harris?"

Her eyes opened slowly, struggling to focus. "Who are you? You don't look like a doctor."

Jamo pulled out his badge, holding it where she could see through the sedative haze. "Detective Jamo. I just want to ask you a few questions about—"

"You're not the boss of me."

And then she was gone, slumping sideways into his arms before he could react. The weight of her—barely anything, bones and skin and pharmaceutical surrender—made something tighten in Jamo's chest. Whatever demons this girl carried, they were eating her alive.

He lowered her back onto the bed, pulled the blanket up, and left the room feeling like he'd failed some test he didn't know he was taking.

What he didn't see—what he couldn't have seen—was the figure crouched on the rooftop across the street. Massive and still as carved stone, watching the hospital window with eyes that burned like dying stars. The Rectifier's gaze never wavered from Christy's sleeping form, even as his mind conjured memories that had no business existing in a demon's consciousness.

The billboard beside him advertised Senator Elizabeth Harris's latest campaign: "A Power for the People." Her face dominated the sign—conservative makeup, political smile, eyes that held all the warmth of a winter lake. The Rectifier stared at those eyes, and something like recognition flickered through whatever passed for his thoughts.

His own eyes closed. The memories came unbidden.

A meadow. 1919. *Summer sun warm on skin that still felt warmth. Willow trees creating shade in patterns of light and dark. And Marybeth, laughing, her face turned upward to catch the sun, her beauty so complete it hurt to witness.*

The memory corrupted. Twisted. The meadow became a church, stone walls closing in. Marybeth no longer laughing but writhing, skin cracking like pottery, eyes blazing with light that wasn't holy, wasn't natural, wasn't anything that should exist in God's creation.

And pain. Such pain. The baptismal font boiling. Holy water turning to steam. His own screams echoing off stone as flesh burned from within, as humanity peeled away like shed skin, as something ancient and terrible crawled into the space where Josef Willem used to live.

The Rectifier's eyes flared.

Below, Jamo emerged from the hospital entrance, joining Brecken on the sidewalk. Their voices carried in the still night air, every word audible to ears that heard more than human sound.

"Shit, she knows more... and probably would've told me everything if we had the time. Damn it!"

"What did you get?"

"She confirmed the second assailant. I didn't get a description, but she mentioned Mickey's over on Seventh."

"What about the killer? Did she say anything about him?"

They moved toward their car. Jamo unlocked the doors, his movements carrying the weight of too many hours without sleep. "All she said was his eyes were fiery and that he saved her. Then she passed out."

The Rectifier rose from his crouch, moving with predatory grace despite his bulk. He passed the Senator Harris billboard, and as he did, something within him—rage or will or the remnants of whatever Josef Willem had been—manifested as heat. The billboard's eyes caught fire, burning out in twin circles of char and melted plastic.

He disappeared into shadows that seemed to welcome him home.

Brecken found Jeff in Exam Room 4, a cast fresh on his arm, eyes red from crying. The boy's mother sat beside him, one hand on his shoulder, protective and worried in equal measure.

"Ma'am, my name is Detective Randall Brecken." He showed his badge. "Is this your son?"

"Yes. This is my son Jeff."

"Is your son the boy that claims to have seen a large man with glowing eyes?"

"No," Jeff said, his voice small but insistent. "They were on fire."

Brecken crouched to the boy's level. Years of investigating had taught him that people—especially children—responded better when you met them at eye level. It removed the intimidation factor, made conversation feel less like interrogation. "You mean they were a bright color? Like yellow contact lenses?"

Tears welled in Jeff's eyes. "No... they had fire coming out of them."

Jeff's mother squeezed his shoulder. "He... he has a big imagination. He doesn't remember how he got here, but he keeps saying the big man in the train yard has his bike."

"You saw this man in a train yard, Jeff?"

"...Yes."

Brecken kept his voice gentle, matter-of-fact. The boy was already frightened. The last thing he needed was an adult telling him he was crazy. "I believe you, Jeff. I believe you."

The relief on the boy's face was immediate and heartbreaking. How many adults had already dismissed his story? How many times had he tried to explain what he'd seen only to be met with patronizing smiles and assumptions about overactive imaginations?

"Can you tell me what happened?" Brecken pulled out his notebook, ready to document whatever came next. "Start from when you went to the train yard."

Jeff wiped his eyes with his good hand. "We... we went to find the thing. Jake said his brother saw it walk through the fence, so we wanted to see. And there was a hole. Like something melted it. The fence was all..." He made a gesture with his good hand, fingers dripping like liquid metal.

"Melted," Brecken said, writing it down.

"Yeah. And we went inside, and Gavin saw a rat, and then we heard this sound. Like... like someone in pain. But big. Really big. And the door just... exploded off the train car." Jeff's words came faster now, reliving the terror. "And

I fell, and my bike broke, and I hurt my arm, and Gavin left me, and then he was there."

"The man with the fiery eyes."

"I looked up at him, and he looked down at me, and..." Jeff trailed off, struggling to articulate something beyond his vocabulary. "It was like he could see everything. Everything I ever thought or did or wanted to do. And I was so scared I passed out."

"But he didn't hurt you."

"No. I woke up here. In the hospital. The doctors said someone brought me in but didn't leave a name."

Brecken wrote this down carefully. An eleven-year-old boy with a broken wrist, delivered anonymously to the ER. The same entity that had decapitated Carlos Javier and incinerated his accomplice had apparently carried this child to safety.

Protector or destroyer? Or somehow both?

Jeff's mother looked at Brecken with the kind of desperation parents get when their children experience something they can't explain or defend against. "Is my son in danger, Detective?"

Brecken wanted to lie. Wanted to give her the reassurance that yes, everything would be fine, the police had everything under control, her boy was safe. But eighteen years as a cop had taught him that lies—even comforting ones—had a way of coming back to bite you.

"I don't know," he said honestly. "But I promise you we're going to figure this out."

Small comfort. But honest. Sometimes that was all you could offer.

Jamo met Brecken at the car, his body language tight with frustration. They slid into their seats—Brecken automatically fastening his seatbelt, Jamo automatically not—and sat in silence for a moment, processing.

High above them, unseen, the Rectifier moved across rooftops with the fluid grace of something that had transcended normal physics. He leaped gaps that should have been impossible, landed with impacts that should have shattered concrete, moved through Detroit's nightscape like a shadow with mass and intention.

"The kid said the same thing," Brecken said finally.

Jamo started the car, his movements mechanical. "Sounds like Dr. Hinkley might be right. Mass hysteria or whatever."

"He also mentioned that he saw the man at an old train yard. His mother said the kids sometimes go over to the abandoned train yard off of 75, near Memorial Park."

"Maybe we should check it out."

"We should try to substantiate their story before we go blazing in there based on the story from a drugged up crazy girl and an eleven year old with an overactive imagination."

Jamo pulled out of the parking spot without responding. The silence between them wasn't hostile, just weighted. They both knew what the evidence suggested. They both knew how insane it sounded. Demons didn't exist. Things with fiery eyes that melted metal and cauterized wounds didn't walk around Detroit protecting drug addicts and delivering injured children to hospitals.

Except apparently they did.

"I'm thinking about going to Mickey's for a drink," Jamo said after several blocks. "You coming?"

"No, I gotta get home to my woman. It's our movie night." Brecken glanced at his partner. "You should go home and take a load off. Jenny always bugs me about how she thinks you work too hard."

"Jesus. Her and Dowling's old lady, they never quit."

"Ever think they may be right?"

"Hard to rest when I know there's demons out there carrying laser guns, chopping off heads with their bare hands and playing Scrabble with internal organs."

Brecken laughed despite himself. "This case keeps getting weirder and weirder... Think you can dump me at my car on the way to Mickey's?"

"I didn't think you would be coming."

They drove through Detroit's nightscape—streetlights creating pools of illumination, abandoned buildings standing like tombstones to better times, the occasional cluster of working businesses hanging on through determination or delusion. This was Jamo's city. Broken, declining, dangerous in ways both mundane and apparently supernatural.

He loved it anyway. Or maybe he just didn't know how to leave.

The precinct parking structure loomed ahead. Jamo pulled in, and Brecken gathered his things—notepad, coffee thermos, the detritus of a working detective's shift.

"Get some rest," Brecken said. "You look like death."

"Feel like it too."

"I'm serious, Jamo. When's the last time you slept more than four hours?"

Jamo thought about it. Actually had to think about it. That was probably answer enough. "I'll sleep when this is solved."

"That's what you always say."

"It's always true."

Brecken climbed out, then leaned back in. "Be careful at Mickey's. Place is full of assholes."

"That's why I'm going. Assholes tend to know things."

Brecken shut the door and headed to his car—a sensible sedan, well-maintained, the automotive equivalent of his personality.

Jamo watched him go, feeling the familiar isolation settle back in. Brecken had Jenny waiting at home. Movie night. Normal life. The kind of life Beth had wanted Jamo to build before she'd realized he couldn't. Wouldn't. Some fundamental part of him was broken in a way that made normal impossible.

Across the street, hidden in shadows on a rooftop, the Rectifier watched. His burning eyes fixed on the Detroit Police Department shield displayed prominently on the building's facade—a knight's shield, heraldic and proud, symbol of protection and service.

The symbol triggered something. Not quite memory. More like echo. Residue of a life that had been Josef Willem's before it became something else.

A barn. Night. 1919. *The smell of hot metal and hay. A boy—young Josef—staring at a shield mounted on the wall, polished to mirror brightness. And a man—the blacksmith, strong hands gentled by affection—placing an arm around the boy's shoulders.*

"That is a symbol of good, son. Men of great valor would tote these shields as protectors of the people."

Young Josef staring at the shield, seeing in its surface not his reflection but his aspiration. To be good. To protect. To serve something greater than himself. How perfectly, how completely, how utterly that dream had been corrupted.

The Rectifier turned away from the police station and disappeared into Detroit's darkness.

***

Mickey's Tavern occupied a building that had probably been charming in the 1950's and had spent the subsequent decades declining into what could generously be called "atmospheric." The sign outside flickered with two dead letters—"Mic y's"—and the windows were tinted dark enough to violate multiple health codes.

Jamo pushed through the door into a familiar wall of smoke, beer, and bodily odors poorly masked by cheap air freshener. Mickey himself stood behind the bar, a barrel-chested man in his fifties who'd probably been handsome once before alcohol and gravity had their way with him.

He saw Jamo and immediately threw down his towel. "What do you want?"

Jamo found a stool. "I'll take a beer and a little info."

"This is bad for business. You can't be hanging around here."

"Answer 'em quick and I'll be out of your hair."

Mickey slid him a beer with the resignation of someone who knew resistance was futile. Jamo took a drink, the cheap lager tasting exactly like every other cheap lager he'd consumed in places like this. "You hear about the alleyway?"

"I'm a bartender. I hear everything."

"Was Carlos Javier hanging in here the other night?"

Mickey's discomfort was immediate and visible. He hesitated, wiping the bar with more attention than it deserved.

"I thought you heard everything."

No response. Jamo took a sip, then slammed the mug down hard enough to make nearby patrons look up. He took a long, deliberate look around the room—taking inventory of faces, noting the various violations and probable warrants represented by Mickey's clientele.

"I see. I'm willing to bet there's all kinds of possession in a place like this."

He started to stand. Mickey's hand shot out. "Okay, okay. He was over in the corner, playing pool with some other fellow I ain't never seen before."

Jamo settled back onto the stool, his expression going carefully blank. "Right."

He spun toward the other patrons. A large biker in head-to-toe black leather sat in the corner, looking annoyed even before Jamo's attention landed on him. "How about you? You look the type to be toting an illegally concealed weapon. Drugs maybe... what else? Probation, warrants..."

The biker stood, unfolding to an impressive height. He loomed over Jamo by at least six inches and probably eighty pounds of muscle and bad intentions. Jamo didn't back down. Just stared into the guy's eyes and smiled.

Then he turned toward a booth where five more bikers sat, all wearing the same colors. "What about you fellas?"

Five hands disappeared under the table. Jamo's hand moved toward his left shoulder, where his service weapon rested in its holster.

"Alright! Alright..." Mickey's voice carried real panic now.

Jamo stepped back, giving everyone room to de-escalate. The big biker sat back down. The five at the booth brought their hands back to visible positions. The moment hung balanced on a knife's edge, then passed.

Jamo returned to his stool. Mickey leaned close, his voice low and urgent. "Rodriguez. Freddy Rodriguez. He's just some runner. Been hanging with Carlos a lot lately."

"A delivery boy. What does he look like?"

"I don't know. About 5'6" maybe, Hispanic, white T-shirt, jeans. He has those corn rows in his hair. He's always hopped up on something when he comes in."

"What time did they head out of here?"

Mickey thought about it. "I dunno, nine, nine thirty or so. Some girl came in, slapped Carlos in the face. She didn't stay. Not too long after that Carlos and Freddy left, too. Freddy kept licking his lips at her and grabbing his dick."

Jamo put down his empty mug. "So, what time did she leave?"

Mickey paused. Jamo swirled his finger for another round. The beer appeared. "Jeez, about five minutes before. 'Bout nine forty-five maybe."

"You didn't find that odd, Mick? Girl gets into it with a dealer, storms out, and five minutes later he follows her?"

Mickey didn't answer. He didn't have to. The silence was admission enough.

"Okay, so they follow her out of here and allegedly drag her into the alley. Anybody else in here that night, shady looking?"

Mickey gave him a look that said the question was ridiculous.

"Nobody with a suit an' tie!"

Jamo surveyed the bar again. Bikers, day laborers, men who looked like they'd made poor life choices and were committed to making more. "Anyone else leave after them?"

"I really wasn't paying attention."

"No," Jamo snapped, "but you remember the girl, Javier, and some other scumbag quite vividly."

Mickey looked cornered, which was exactly where Jamo wanted him. "She was a pretty hot chick, man."

Jamo's expression hardened. Mickey raised his hands defensively. "Look, once they leave my door, I got nothing to do with it."

"Out of sight out of mind, huh?"

"What you do in here is my business, what you do out there is yours. Isn't that when you're supposed to come in, Detective... serve and protect and all that?"

"You must be confused like everyone else. It means serve and protect the Constitution of the United States. Not give rides to drunks and junkies because they can't afford a cab."

Mickey actually laughed. "Ha!"

"We can't be everywhere all the time, Mickey. That's why we rely on upstanding citizens like yourself and your fine patrons..." Jamo waved generally toward the collection of probable felons occupying the bar stools.

"I forthwith'd, Detective. Now can I get back to being the upright citizen I was before you came in?"

Jamo pulled out a card and wrote on it—his direct line, case number, the expectation of cooperation. He slid it to Mickey. "Yeah, sure, as long as you provide the great city of Detroit with your full statement."

Mickey grumbled but took the card.

"Make sure it's accurate and full of detail, Mickey! I'll be back if it isn't."

Jamo stood and headed for the door. The big biker flipped him off as he passed. Jamo nodded back, acknowledging the gesture with professional courtesy.

"What about your drinks?" Mickey called after him.

Jamo paused at the door. "What drinks? I'm on duty."

He walked out. Behind him, Mickey's voice carried clearly: "Dick."

The parking lot behind Mickey's was poorly lit—one working streetlight casting long shadows, broken glass crunching underfoot, the smell of stale beer and human waste marking it as a place where bad things happened regularly.

Jamo found a pathway connecting the lot to the bottom end of the alleyway where Carlos Javier had been murdered. Police tape lay on the ground, torn from its moorings by wind or curious passersby.

He stepped past it into shadows that seemed deeper than they should be. The alley was littered with the archaeology of addiction—drug vials, broken syringes, burnt spoons, the scattered evidence of people trying to escape reality through chemistry.

He came to the area where Javier's body had been found. The blood was long gone, washed away by rain or absorbed into ancient asphalt. But the spot felt marked anyway. Haunted, maybe, though Jamo didn't believe in ghosts.

At least he hadn't. Before this case.

A rustling sound came from above. Jamo looked up, his hand moving automatically toward his weapon. A pigeon fluttered away, passing by something in the shadows that was definitely not a pigeon. Something much larger. Much more still.

Jamo pulled out his small flashlight and aimed it upward. The fire escape overlooked the murder scene, metal railings catching the light. Something about them looked wrong. He moved closer, trying to get a better angle.

His foot scuffed against something on the ground.

Jamo aimed the flashlight down. A glob of metal, melted and resolidified, stuck to the asphalt at the toe of his shoe. He crouched, examining it more closely. Definitely metal. Iron or steel, maybe. Melted at temperatures that required serious heat.

Another smaller glob sat a few feet away. He tried to pick it up. It wouldn't budge, fused to the asphalt like it had been part of the original pour.

Jamo stood and shined the flashlight back at the fire escape. The bent railings caught the light at an angle that revealed scorch marks. The metal had been heated to the point of malleability, then cooled in warped positions. The color matched the globs on the ground.

He pulled out his cell phone and switched to camera mode. The flash illuminated the fire escape in stark white light. He aimed down at the globs. Another flash.

The light revealed the bikers from Mickey's bar surrounding him.

Jamo barely had time to register their presence before something hard and heavy—a bat—struck him from behind. His knees buckled. He fell forward into a knee that caught him square in the face. Cartilage crunched. Blood filled his mouth.

He went down hard. Boots materialized from every direction, stomping, kicking, aimed at ribs and kidneys and head. Jamo tried to cover his face, tried to roll away, tried to reach for his gun.

His holster was empty.

Someone had already taken it. Of course they had. Bikers might be criminals, but they weren't stupid.

Another kick connected with his ribs. Something cracked—bones or cartilage or both. Jamo caught a glimpse of the bat being raised again, then a streak of golden light, and then nothing.

Darkness.

But not for long.

The biker with the bat pulled back for what he intended to be the killing blow. The bat rose. Descended.

And stopped.

It was stuck. Held by something invisible. And getting hot. Very hot. The aluminum began to glow, red transitioning to orange transitioning to white. The biker screamed and tried to let go, but the bat had already melted onto his hand, fusing with flesh and bone.

He was yanked upward with impossible force, his flaming body arcing through the air like a comet. He landed on the rooftop forty feet above, his screams cutting off abruptly.

Another biker started screaming. He looked down at his stomach, where his leather jacket and shirt were smoking. Then his stomach simply opened, flames shooting out as if someone had unzipped him from the inside. He flew backward, propelled by force or fear, and slammed into the dumpster with a hollow boom.

The remaining two bikers froze, trying to process what they were witnessing. One broke first, turning to run.

The side of his face burst into flames. Not from external fire—from within. His skin split, revealing something that glowed underneath. His scream was interrupted when an invisible force slammed his head into the brick wall. The skull detonated like a melon, flaming chunks sticking to the wall as his body collapsed.

The last biker ran.

He made it maybe twenty feet before two points of golden fire appeared in his peripheral vision. He looked up, seeing something that his brain refused to process, something so far outside normal experience that his mind simply shut down.

The Rectifier leaped.

The impact was seismic. The biker's body was driven into the asphalt with enough force to crack pavement, his organs liquifying from the sudden deceleration, his death instantaneous and absolute.

The Rectifier stood slowly, his massive form silhouetted against the distant streetlight. His face was a horror of cracks and fissures, glowing from within like cooling lava. His hands radiated heat that made the air shimmer.

He turned toward Jamo's unconscious body and walked forward with deliberate steps. Each footfall left a scorch mark on the asphalt.

He knelt beside the detective, studying him with eyes that burned like small suns. Jamo's face was a mess—broken nose, split eyebrow, jaw already swelling. But alive. Still breathing. Still salvageable.

The Rectifier's gaze fell on the police shield attached to Jamo's belt. The symbol triggered something deep in whatever remained of Josef Willem's consciousness. Not quite recognition. More like resonance.

Fire. So much fire. A girl's voice screaming—not Marybeth, someone else, someone younger. Jamo reaching through flames, his hands blistering, his left side catching fire, his clothes melting into his skin. Reaching for her anyway. Reaching even as the floor collapsed, even as she fell, even as everything burned.

From within darkness, two eyes opened. Golden. Burning. Filled with rage that had no outlet, with guilt that had no absolution, with a need to protect that had been twisted into a curse.

The eyes erupted into blinding fire.

The Rectifier straightened. He couldn't save Jamo—not directly. Couldn't carry him to safety without burning him alive. The heat that flowed through his hands would cook flesh before it could heal. Whatever protective instinct drove him had limits imposed by his nature.

But he could do something.

He moved toward the open window of a nearby building—Jamo's apartment building, he realized, following some instinct he didn't understand. The fire escape beckoned. He climbed with grace that belied his bulk, metal groaning and warping under his touch.

Jamo's window. Unlocked. The Rectifier forced it open, leaving scorch marks on the frame. He climbed inside, his burning presence filling the small spare room with heat and light.

An easel stood by the window. An unfinished painting of Saint Anthony's Cathedral rested on it—accurate in every detail except for the final elements. The Rectifier studied it with something that might have been appreciation. Or recognition. Or grief.

He found Jamo's palette and favorite brush. And then, moving with inhuman precision, he completed the painting. Every shadow. Every line. Every detail that Jamo's exhausted mind had captured but his exhausted body hadn't yet transferred to canvas.

When it was finished, the Rectifier stood back. The painting was perfect. A photographic record of horror rendered in oils.

He turned and climbed back through the window, leaving more scorch marks on the sill. On the railing. Evidence of his presence for anyone who knew to look.

Below, in the alley, Jamo began to stir.

The Rectifier descended quickly, reaching the ground as the detective's eyes fluttered open. He moved back into shadows, watching as Jamo struggled to his feet, stumbled, nearly fell.

Jamo looked around, seeing the bodies. The scorch marks. The evidence of violence beyond human capacity. His hand went to his empty holster. His eyes widened.

Then he turned and walked—staggered, really—away from the alley. Back toward his apartment. Toward safety.

The Rectifier watched him go.

Then he turned and disappeared into Detroit's darkness, returning to the abandoned train yard where he'd been hiding. Where he'd been waiting. Where memories of Marybeth and guilt over a hundred years of servitude and something like hope had been building toward something he didn't yet understand.

The night swallowed him whole.

And in her hospital bed, Christy Harris slept on, protected by something she couldn't see, hunted by powers she didn't comprehend, caught in a war that had started long before her birth...

That would end—one way or another—in fire.

CHAPTER 4

THE MAN WITH THE RED-SASH

The Rectifier's hands moved across the rusted metal wall with surprising delicacy. Each brushstroke released a thin trail of smoke where heat met paint, but the image taking shape beneath his touch was beautiful. Heartbreaking, really, if anyone had been there to appreciate the tragedy of a demon painting from memory.

Marybeth's face emerged from darkness—the curve of her smile, the light in her eyes, the way her hair caught summer sun. The Rectifier worked in silence broken only by the hiss of burning paint, creating something that shouldn't exist. A demon's tribute to lost humanity.

He paused, brush suspended in mid-stroke, and closed his eyes against pain that had nothing to do with physical sensation.

The memory came unbidden, relentless.

A church basement in 1919. *Modest furnishings. A simple desk bearing leather-bound books, ink, and pen. And an easel where Father Josef Willem—still human, still innocent—painted the woman he loved.*

Sunlight through the small window blessed the canvas with warmth. The painting captured Marybeth perfectly—her beauty, her spirit, the way she made the world feel possible despite all evidence to the contrary.

Then corruption. Black lines snaking across the painted face like cracks in porcelain. The eyes burning from within. The background bleeding to crimson darkness. And behind Marybeth's head, the symbol of Flauros forming in blood-red accusation.

The painting catching fire. Willem backing away. The room transforming.

Suddenly he stood in a farmhouse bedroom. Marybeth before him, but not Marybeth. Not anymore. Tied to a chair, writhing, singing in tongues that predated language, her voice carrying the weight of ancient malice.

The song spoke of hunting. Of consuming. Of Saint Sebastian's bloodline traced through centuries, found at last, ready for destruction.

Marybeth's face changed. Skin cracking like drought-stricken earth. Eyes glazing yellow. Her body moving with serpentine grace that human joints shouldn't allow.

Willem—still Willem, not yet the Rectifier—held a Bible where his paintbrush had been. Holy water instead of turpentine. He recited the rite of exorcism with tears streaming down his face, knowing even as he spoke the words that they wouldn't work. That this was trap, not possession. That he'd been played from the beginning.

The holy water hit Marybeth's face and boiled away to steam.

She stopped writhing. Stopped singing. Looked at him with eyes that held momentary clarity, as if the woman he loved surfaced one final time through demonic occupation.

"I love you, Willem... I'm sorry."

Her voice beautiful. Heartbreaking. True.

And then it changed. Became something else. The last word "sorry" transforming mid-syllable into a guttural bellow that shook the farmhouse walls.

Her jaw snapped. Her mouth stretched wide, tearing at the corners. Eyes turned black, then erupted with fire from within—not metaphorical fire, but actual flames that cooked her from the inside out and burst through her sockets like acetylene torches.

Her head whipped wildly, spraying fire and white light across the room. Then it stopped. Locked on Willem.

The demon wearing Marybeth's body smiled.

And Father Josef Willem flew backward into the wall with enough force to crack plaster. His face split open—literally split—fissures forming across skin as something terrible pushed outward from within. Boiling blood leaked from the crevices.

He screamed. Opened his eyes. Fire shot out.

The Rectifier was being born.

The brush fell from his hand, clattering on the rusted floor of the rail car. The Rectifier opened his eyes—burning eyes, demon eyes—and stared at the painting he'd created. Marybeth smiled back at him from the wall, forever young, forever beautiful, forever lost.

He turned away and disappeared into the shadows of the abandoned train yard, carrying Jamo's palette and brush like relics from a life he could no longer claim.

Jamo limped into the morgue feeling like he'd been run over by something industrial and possibly malevolent. Every step sent fresh pain through ribs he was certain were cracked. His face throbbed. His head pounded. His memory of the previous night existed only in fragments—Mickey's bar, the alley, violence, and then nothing until he'd woken up in his own bed, fully clothed and mysteriously alive.

Dr. Chen looked up from the body she was examining and stopped mid-motion. "Morning, Detective... holy shit! Who ran over you?"

"Let's not go there." Jamo approached the examination table, moving like a man three times his age. "Got something?"

"Take a look at these."

She led him to a metal table bearing a dish he really didn't want to examine more closely. The contents looked back at him with the accusatory quality of internal organs removed from their proper context.

"Uh... sorry, I already ate."

"Not the stomach, it's what was in it..."

Chen handed him a collection of plastic evidence bags containing photographs. Jamo examined them with growing unease. The images showed Father Paul—younger, healthier, still alive—sitting on a bed next to a young girl. Maybe nine or ten years old. Blonde hair. Scared eyes.

"These were in his stomach?"

"That and a few were still lodged in his throat." Chen pointed to several crumpled photographs on the table, slimy with digestive fluid.

"So the priest swallowed them?"

"Well, by the looks of the abrasions in his mouth and esophagus they were forced down."

Jamo flipped one of the photos over. A date stamp on the back, slightly faded: 2/22/87.

"No burn marks," he muttered.

"What?"

"Nothing." Jamo studied the date. "These were taken in '87... if this girl is still alive she'd probably be in her twenties."

"Possibly. The girl looks to be somewhere around nine or ten."

"Is it possible that Father Paul forced these down his own throat?"

Chen considered this. "Maybe, as an act of desperation?"

"Desperation?"

"What's the easiest way to get rid of something quickly?"

The logic was sound, horrible but sound. "He was trying to hide them. But why?" Jamo moved toward the body cooler. "Which one of these is him?"

"Eight."

Jamo pulled open drawer eight and yanked out Father Paul's remains. The body had deteriorated further since the initial examination—skin discolored, flesh settling in ways that emphasized its absence of life. He pulled back the sheet.

"No burn marks," he said to himself, studying the photographs again.

These photos hadn't been burned. Hadn't been seared with the symbol of Flauros. Hadn't been part of the trail leading to the altar. These were different. Hidden. Important enough that Father Paul had tried to destroy them even as he died.

"You say something?" Chen asked.

Jamo didn't answer. He was already moving toward the exit, his mind racing through connections he didn't fully understand yet. The doors swung shut behind him, leaving Chen staring at the space where he'd been.

The precinct buzzed with afternoon energy when Jamo finally arrived. Brecken sat at his desk, typing with the focused intensity of someone trying to catch up on paperwork before the next crisis interrupted.

"You're late," Brecken said without looking up. "I figured you were out at Mickey's till whenever, so I gave Michaels a bullshit story that you had a meeting."

"Ugh. Actually I did, with the Medical Examiner."

Jamo collapsed into his chair with a groan that sounded older than his years. Brecken kept typing, still not looking up.

"He went off on a tirade about you and how lately you're mixing cases up or something. What, did you tie one on last night?"

"Might as well have." Jamo grabbed his head, wincing. "I don't remember getting home. Holy fuck, my head."

Brecken finally looked up. His expression shifted from casual annoyance to genuine concern in a heartbeat. "Shit! What happened to you?"

"I'm fine."

"What the hell happened?"

"I'm not even sure I know... I went to Mickey's and ended up getting jumped by a bunch of scumbags..."

Brecken reached for the phone. Jamo hung it up before he could dial.

"Look, Randy, I'm fine."

But he wasn't fine. Not really. As he sat there, rubbing the back of his head, fragments of memory surfaced. The bikers surrounding him. The bat coming down. Pain. And then... something else. Something his brain refused to fully process.

Heat. Incredible heat. And golden light.

Screaming that wasn't his own.

The sensation of being watched by something that cared whether he lived or died.

"You sure you're okay, buddy?"

Jamo blinked, snapping back to the present. "Yeah, don't worry about me."

"What did Mickey have to say?"

"That I wasn't serving or protecting enough."

"Seriously, anything?"

"Freddy Rodriguez. Can you look him up? See if we got an address or license plate for this guy... 5'6", average, Hispanic, has cornrows..."

Brecken turned to his computer and started clicking. Jamo pulled out his phone and scrolled through the photos from last night. The melted metal globs. The warped fire escape. And then the painting—his painting of Saint Anthony's Cathedral, somehow finished despite the fact that he'd been unconscious.

Or had he? Was it possible he'd staggered home, climbed the fire escape, and completed the painting in some fugue state before collapsing into bed?

Except there were scorch marks on the window frame. On the sill. On the railing.

Handprints made of heat.

"125 Holbrook..."

Jamo scrolled to the photo of the finished painting and stared at it. Something was wrong. Something about the details that shouldn't be there. He grabbed the crime scene photos from his desk and compared them.

"There's a felony warrant out on this guy," Brecken said, excited.

Jamo studied both images. The painting showed something the crime scene photo didn't. A door. Behind the altar, slightly to the right. Hidden or disguised in the actual crime scene, but clearly visible in the painting.

How had he known to paint it there?

His phone rang: CAPTAIN MICHAELS.

"Jamo... OK, we'll be there in a sec."

Yelling erupted from the other end loud enough for Brecken to hear. Jamo closed the phone.

"We'll be where in a sec?"

***

Captain Michaels stood behind his desk like a man preparing for battle or stroke, possibly both. His face had achieved a shade of red that suggested cardiovascular concerns. Jamo and Brecken sat before him like students called to the principal's office, which wasn't far from the truth.

"I don't know what the fuck happened to your face and I don't know what the fuck you were thinking going to that hospital!" Michaels's voice carried the kind of volume that made people in adjacent offices pause their conversations. "I feel like I'm giving a speech to my kids about doing what you're told. I said don't go over there and what happens?"

Jamo opened his mouth to respond.

"I get a fuckin' phone call saying there were two of my men seen harassing the exact girl I ordered not to bother. Why?"

Jamo's lips moved. Michaels didn't let him speak.

"What do you want me to do when I get phone calls threatening my job if I don't deal with you two?"

They sat in silence, staring at their captain, waiting to see if this was rhetorical or if he actually wanted answers.

"Well?!"

"Oh," Jamo said, "you want us to answer that one?"

"Jesus, Jamo. This is some serious shit. These people have all the connections to seriously fuck us over."

"I didn't realize Senator Harris had such a fondness for the Department."

Michaels finally sat down, the anger draining into something more like resignation. "Don't be a smart ass. You guys obviously know what we're up against. These people don't mess around. Here's something you don't know... as of this morning, if you two are seen anywhere in the proximity of this girl, I've been asked to have you both suspended. Indefinitely."

"I don't need this." Jamo stood, wincing, and headed for the door.

"Look, Jamo..."

Jamo grabbed the handle.

"Jamo, wait..."

He turned, his hand still on the doorknob.

"I'm on your side. I don't like this any more than you do. I've never in all my years seen such a blatant abuse of power in person."

"So where does that leave us?"

"They're the ones pulling the strings on this one, legally. I'd hate to see it ruin any careers."

Jamo walked out without responding. Brecken started to follow, but Michaels motioned him back down. They talked in low voices while Jamo stood in the hallway, trying to process the implications.

Senator Elizabeth Harris. Political powerhouse. Mother of Christy Harris. Woman with enough influence to shut down a murder investigation with a phone call.

Why?

What was she protecting?

Or more accurately: who was she protecting?

Brecken emerged from the office a minute later. "Jamo, wait up."

They walked back to their desks in silence. Jamo sat and pulled out his phone again, staring at the painting. Brecken settled into his chair with a sigh.

"Michaels said he was going to handle it. He just wants us to do our job and be more careful. He asked about your face."

"Yeah?"

"He said it was an improvement."

Jamo forced a smile that felt like moving broken glass. He went back to studying the painting photo, comparing it to the crime scene images.

"So what's up with you lately, anyway?" Brecken asked.

"What are you talking about?"

"You seem preoccupied or something."

Jamo kept his eyes on the phone screen. The door in the painting stood out now that he'd noticed it. Clear as day. How had he known?

"Seriously, man, it's like this job is under your skin. Did you forget something yesterday?"

Brecken slid Jamo's service weapon across the desk. The gun he'd been wearing when the bikers jumped him. The gun that should still be in that alley or in evidence or stolen or anywhere except back on Brecken's desk.

"I'm fine."

But he wasn't fine. Someone—something—had brought him home. Had returned his weapon. Had finished his painting. Had saved his life.

The thing with fiery eyes.

"I hate this place sometimes," Jamo muttered, holstering his gun and trying not to think about impossible things.

Brecken made a phone call. "Hey, it's Detective Brecken. Listen, can you have a black-and-white pick up a Francis J. Rodriguez? 125 Holbrook. Yeah... What's that?"

Jamo noticed something in the painting photo. Something he'd missed before. A detail in the shadows that shouldn't be there.

"You have SWAT dispatched to that residence for a situation? What type of situation? Jesus, they don't move until I get there!"

Brecken gathered his things with practiced speed. "We gotta move. They got a potential hostage situation involving our boy Rodriguez."

Jamo stared at the photograph. At the shadow in the painting that looked almost like a figure. Watching. Waiting.

"Actually, can you hit that one on your own?"

"You got something?"

"I'm not sure what it is yet, but it's something."

Saint Anthony's

The Cathedral stood empty in the late afternoon light, stained glass windows casting pools of color across abandoned pews. The police tape across the entrance hung loose, one end torn free by wind or vandals. Jamo ducked under it and pushed through the heavy oak doors.

Inside, silence pressed down like physical weight. The cathedral felt different without the chaos of crime scene investigation—more sacred, maybe, or just more aware of the violation that had occurred within its walls.

Jamo made his way to the altar, his footsteps echoing off stone. He pulled out his phone and opened the painting photo, then looked around for the angle that matched the image.

He found it near the front pew and sat down, studying the photo. The door should be visible from here. Behind the altar, to the right. But when he looked up, he saw only ornate wood paneling. No door. No opening.

Nothing noticeable.

He took a deep breath—winced at the pain in his ribs—and breathed out slowly. Pulled the crime scene photo from his pocket and compared it to the painting.

"What the fuck..."

The painting showed details the crime scene photo didn't. Shadows in slightly different positions.

Light falling at a subtly different angle. And the door, clear as day in the painted image, completely invisible in the photographic one.

Jamo stood and started pacing, trying to work through the logic. Someone had finished his painting. That person had included a door that didn't appear in any crime scene documentation. Which meant either:

A) Someone had invented the door from imagination, or

B) Someone knew about a door that investigators had missed.

Option B seemed more likely. Which raised uncomfortable questions about who had been in his apartment and how they knew about hidden doors in churches.

The thing with fiery eyes.

The Rectifier.

Jamo walked to the altar and examined the wall where the painted door should be. Wood paneling, old and elaborate, covered the entire surface. He ran his hands across it, looking for seams or irregularities.

His fingers caught on loose molding. He moved it aside and found a keyhole hidden beneath.

Locked.

He knocked on the wall. Hollow.

He tried to push it open. It didn't budge.

Jamo backed up, taking a deep breath that sent pain lancing through his damaged ribs. Then he kicked.

The door exploded inward with a crack of splintering wood. Jamo stumbled through, groaning, and found himself in a large study.

His flashlight illuminated rows of bookshelves, a substantial desk, and all the trappings of scholarly pursuit. He moved to the shelves and pulled down a book at random.

The pages were blank.

Another book. Also blank.

"What the...?"

Every book on the shelf was fake—elaborate props, covers and bindings with nothing inside. Jamo turned to the desk.

A Bible sat prominently displayed. Papers scattered across the surface. A half-burned candle in a brass holder. He rifled through the papers—parish records, correspondence, nothing immediately relevant. The Bible had passages highlighted and notes in the margins, but nothing jumped out as significant.

The drawers yielded office supplies and files. Jamo sifted through them, finding nothing.

He sat in Father Paul's chair and sighed, looking around the hidden study. Why all the fake books? What was the point of this elaborate deception?

His eyes fell on writing carved into the wood inside the desk's well. He pointed his flashlight at it.

Selah 32:7.

Excited now, he grabbed a pen and wrote the reference on his hand. Then he found the Bible and flipped to Psalms. There it was, highlighted: "Thou art my hiding place; thou shalt preserve me from trouble; thou shalt compass me about with songs of deliverance."

"Just like in the movies," Jamo muttered, running his hand along the underside of the desk.

His fingers found a button. Click.

A hidden compartment shimmied open beneath the desk. Inside: an old folder wrapped with rope, a journal of meeting minutes, and a VHS tape with "Christy" written on the label in faded marker.

Jamo gathered everything carefully, his detective's instincts screaming that he'd just found something important. Possibly case-breaking. Definitely dangerous.

He left the study, walked through the cathedral, and emerged into fading daylight just as a cloaked figure emerged from the shadows behind the altar.

The Red-Sashed Man stood in the study doorway, holding an old leather-bound book that Jamo hadn't noticed. He watched the detective leave, then followed at a distance, moving with the silent grace of someone who'd spent a lifetime learning not to be seen.

In his hands, the book felt warm. Alive. Ready.

Everything was proceeding according to plan.

A plan one hundred years in the making.

A plan that would culminate on July 15th.

Tonight.

The hospital room smelled like antiseptic and fear. Freddy Rodriguez lay in the bed, bandaged and unconscious, connected to an IV that dripped pain medication and antibiotics. A uniformed officer sat in a chair by the door, reading a magazine with the dedication of someone paid to be bored.

Brecken stood in the hallway with Jamo, keeping his voice low. "What happened to him? You were supposed to question him, not put him in the freakin' hospital!"

"He took a nose dive from the second story."

Jamo gave him a look.

"Without my help. Something spooked him, he tried to off himself."

Jamo handed Brecken an envelope containing the materials from Father Paul's study. Brecken opened it and looked inside.

"What's this?"

"There's a tape inside and an old journal."

"Where did you find this stuff?"

"I... doesn't matter now. We need to find out what's on this tape."

Brecken pulled out the VHS tape and examined the label. "Christy."

"Yeah. That's what I'm afraid of."

They found a nurse—young, attractive, wearing a name tag that read LISA—and convinced her to let them use the staff library. She wheeled in a cart with a TV and combination VCR/DVD player, then lingered near Jamo with the kind of interest that suggested professional concern crossing into personal territory.

"Who dressed your bandages?" She studied his battered face.

Jamo touched his brow. "Uh... I did."

She smiled. "I can tell. If you want I can take a look at those and put fresh dressings on for you."

"Probably a good idea. Let me just take a look at this real quick?"

Lisa checked her watch. "I have to do my rounds now anyway. Come see me when you're done."

"Thanks."

"Anything for the good guys."

She walked out, and Jamo found himself admiring her figure in a way that felt inappropriate given the circumstances. Brecken chuckled.

"She's young enough to be your daughter."

"Too bad we don't have time to find out."

They loaded the tape and sat back. The screen filled with static, then resolved into grainy surveillance footage of a bedroom.

Young Father Paul entered the frame, guiding a little girl toward the bed. She looked scared. Possibly drugged. She was maybe nine or ten years old, with blonde hair and features that might—might—match Christy Harris.

"Christy, come here, we're going to have another lesson," Father Paul said off-screen.

Jamo turned to Brecken. "You gotta be fucking kidding me."

"You think it's the Harris girl?"

"It kind of looks like her. It's definitely the same place as the photos the Medical Examiner pulled out of the priest's stomach."

On screen, the girl spoke: "It makes me feel bad."

"I understand, but this is very important, dear."

"I know, it's our secret, right."

Father Paul walked back into frame and sat on the bed next to her. Put his arm around her shoulders.

Jamo hit pause. "I can't watch this. You think you can sit through it, be my guest. I just... I can't."

"He might end up saying something to shed a little light on this fucked-up case."

"Good. Tails you win. I'll meet you back here in a few."

"What are you going to do?"

"I figure I can use the time to speak with our victim."

Brecken sighed and pulled out the journal as Jamo left. He hit play and forced himself to watch, taking notes, looking for anything that might explain this nightmare.

***

The psychiatric floor had different security than the regular hospital. Jamo showed his badge to the desk attendant—a tall blond guy named Jake—and noticed the sign-in sheet.

B. HARRIS had visited C. HARRIS in room 523. Signed in at 6:47 p.m., signed out at 7:15 p.m.

Visiting hours ran from 10 a.m. to 9 p.m., so Senator Harris's visit was technically allowed. But something about it felt wrong. The timing. The brief duration. The fact that she'd come at all.

Jake buzzed him through. Jamo found room 823 and knocked before entering.

Christy turned as he walked in. Her eyes were sunken, ringed with darkness that spoke of withdrawal and fear and sleepless nights. She looked surprised and relieved when she saw him.

"Ms. Harris, I need to ask you a few more questions."

Christy took a seat, staring at the floor. "He... he's here, isn't he?"

Jamo paused. "It's safe, he's in custody and under a watch."

She looked up, confused, focused on his eyes. "What?"

"Freddy Rodriguez, one of the assailants from the alleyway."

Distant look. Fear creeping back in.

"Do you remember anything about the other night in the alleyway? Who did that to Carlos?"

Christy grew fearful. She moved to her bed and sat, staring blankly at the wall. "I... I... I don't remember."

"People are getting killed..."

She shook her head, tears assembling.

Jamo took a knee, adopting a sympathetic approach. "Listen, I know you have problems. I can promise you that you're not in any trouble. I just want—"

"It's not that... He's like my guardian angel. Something has always been out there protecting me."

"You mean like your mother's security people?"

"No. It's always been this way. Always seems like whenever someone would hurt me they'd get hurt... sometimes bad, or just disappear."

Jamo felt ice crawl up his spine. "Is that what happened to Father Paul? Did he hurt you?"

Christy's eyes went wide. Tears streamed down her face. "Father Paul... What's wrong with Father Paul?"

Jamo considered his words carefully. "He's dead."

She broke down. Sobbing. Real grief that couldn't be faked. "Why? What happened?!"

"He was murdered. By the same guy who killed Carlos in that alley."

She wiped her eyes, looked away, stared at the wall again. Shaking.

"Please... tell me what you know. Who is killing these people?"

Long pause. Then: "I think I've seen him in my dreams. The thing I saw in that alleyway... He's always the same in my dream. Dark and shadowy. His burning eyes. My mother used to tell me bedtime stories about him. That I shouldn't be afraid of him and he would never hurt me. She always said that I had nothing to worry about because he would always protect me. My grandmother told my mother the same stories."

"Who is he?"

"I... don't know."

"So you believe that this... thing killed these people because he is protecting you?"

"I know it sounds crazy, but it's always been that way since I can remember. Except I always thought it was just some spiritual thing. I hadn't ever seen him before. Before the other night in the alley, I never believed he actually existed."

"You're telling me that this kind of thing has been happening to you your whole life?"

"I've never spoken about it before. Not even to my mother. There's been a lot of people in my life that have either been hurt or disappeared after they've done something bad to me. I've always thought it was just karma. I would dream about revenge and then it would happen. I've been seeing him a lot lately, but never in person. In my dreams, I mean. It would usually only happen every so often, but ever since my mother told me about Father Paul..."

She started tearing up again.

"Were you close to him?"

Disdain crossed her features. "I was... until mother told me about how he... I don't remember it..."

She got up, ran to the bathroom, and threw up. Jamo heard her retching, heard her slide to the floor. When she emerged, she sat on the toilet, curled into herself.

He got her water. She drank, coughed.

"Did he, Father Paul, ever..."

Christy curled into a ball and began to sob.

"I'm sorry," Jamo said quietly, and left.

He stood in the hallway, hands shaking, trying to process what he'd just learned. Senator Harris had told her daughter that Father Paul had abused her. Had planted memories or suspicions or outright lies. Had turned Christy against the one person who might have saved her.

Why?

The uniformed officer still sat by Rodriguez's door, looking bored.

"He awake yet?"

"Not the last time I checked."

Lisa appeared from a nearby room, smiling when she saw Jamo. "You want me to look at those cuts for you?"

"Sure. Just take it easy on me."

She examined his brow, her touch gentle and professional. "I can clean this up and put a fresh bandage on it. It might need a stitch or two. You'll have to go downstairs for that."

The officer looked over. "You get those on the job?"

"Yeah, and what feels like a few busted ribs, too."

Lisa's expression shifted to concern. "Broken ribs? Let me see."

Jamo backed away. "Uh, it's fine. I'll be fine. I don't think they're broken. Bruised maybe."

"Let me take a look just to be sure."

"No, that's okay. Really."

She got the message and backed off.

"Stop being so spleeny."

Then she stopped, making a face. "What's burning?"

Jamo smelled it too. He saw over the officer's shoulder a yellow flickering from behind Rodriguez's room window.

He charged into the room, followed by the officer and Lisa, and stopped.

Freddy Rodriguez was on fire.

Not externally. From within. His chest glowed like a furnace, cracks forming in his skin, light bleeding through like lava through cooling rock. His eyes opened—burning eyes, golden eyes—and he screamed.

The scream wasn't human.

The room erupted into chaos. Fire alarms shrieked. Sprinklers activated. The officer grabbed Lisa and pulled her back as Rodriguez sat up, flames spreading across his hospital gown.

Jamo stared, unable to move, unable to process what he was witnessing.

The symbol of Flauros appeared on Rodriguez's chest, burning itself into flesh from the inside out.

And in the doorway, visible for just a moment before disappearing into shadow, stood a figure in a dark cloak with a red sash.

Watching.

Satisfied.

Gone.

Rodriguez's screaming stopped. He collapsed back onto the bed, his body cooling to ash, the symbol still glowing faintly on what remained of his chest.

The sprinklers continued to rain down.

The alarms continued to shriek.

And Jamo stood frozen, staring at the evidence that this case had moved far beyond anything he could explain, contain, or solve using conventional methods.

Something was protecting Christy Harris.

Something was killing anyone who hurt her.

And tonight—July 15th—something was going to happen that would make everything up to this point look like a warmup.

He just had to figure out what before it was too late.

CHAPTER 5
THE ABANDONED RAIL YARD

F reddy Rodriguez was already dead when the fire reached him. That was the only mercy in what happened next.

Jamo charged into the hospital room, the uniformed officer and Lisa close behind. Wind billowed the curtains near the window—portions of the fabric edges smoking, small flames dancing along the hem. Behind the privacy curtain that divided the room, Freddy's silhouette flickered and danced in grotesque shadow-play.

Jamo grabbed the curtain and yanked it aside.

What remained of Freddy Rodriguez sat upright in bed, his face carved away as if someone had used a super-heated ice cream scoop to remove everything from his bottom lip to his hairline. No skin. No muscle. No eyes. Just a gaping cavity of cauterized flesh, smoking and sizzling, the bone beneath it charred black.

His groin had received similar treatment—a gaping hole of seared tissue, the sheets and fabric around it still burning with lazy orange flames.

Lisa made a sound behind him. Not quite a scream. More like all the air leaving her lungs at once.

Jets in the ceiling activated, blasting CO2 with a pneumatic shriek. The alarm system wailed. Freddy's burning groin extinguished. The window curtains went out, leaving only smoke and the acrid smell of burned flesh.

Jamo pushed Lisa toward the officer. "Get her out of here! Seal this place off!"

The officer grabbed Lisa and pulled her toward the hallway. She went without resistance, her professional composure shattered by what she'd witnessed.

Jamo turned back to the room and noticed the window. A large hole in the glass—not broken, melted. The edges were smooth, resolidified from liquid back to solid in warped waves.

He took a step forward. Something crunched under his foot.

Mounds of melted glass—clear and black—littered the floor and window sill. Still warm. Still slightly pliable.

Jamo leaned out the window and looked up.

Two white eyes stared back at him, burning like stars.

The Rectifier's hand shot out and grabbed Jamo's shoulder—right where the old burn scar tissue was thickest, most sensitive. The touch ignited something in Jamo's nervous system. Not quite pain. Not quite sensation. Something else.

His body spasmed.

And then he was somewhere else.

Watching Christy through the Rectifier's eyes. Following her from rooftops and shadows. Seeing her walk to her car, go to bed, do drugs in bathrooms that reeked of desperation. Watching her have loveless sex with men whose faces blurred together into a catalog of transactions.

The Rectifier growing sad. Not angry. Sad. The emotion bleeding through the connection with unexpected intensity.

Christy walking into Mickey's tavern. Walking out. Javier and Rodriguez following her into the alley. Trying to rape her.

The Rectifier descending like judgment incarnate. Javier's head igniting from within. The neck cauterizing as the skull separated. Rodriguez running.

Watching Jamo talk to Christy in the examination room that first time. Studying the detective's face. Seeing something there. Recognition? Kinship?

Following Jamo to the police precinct. Seeing the shield on the building—that symbol of protection and service. Something stirring in what passed for the Rectifier's memory. A boy staring at a knight's shield in a barn. A voice saying: "Men of great valor would tote these shields as protectors of the people."

Watching Jamo walk out of Mickey's. Following him into the alley. The bikers attacking. Jamo falling. The Rectifier killing them all—quick, brutal, necessary. Carrying Jamo's unconscious body back to his apartment. Climbing the fire escape. Laying him in bed.

Seeing the unfinished painting. Understanding what it meant. Taking brush and palette. Finishing it. Every detail perfect. Every shadow precise.

Then the images intensified, became less discernible—

A railroad sign. Brecken unconscious and bleeding, cradled in burning hands. Jamo getting married to a woman who wasn't Beth. Jamo dying of old age, surrounded by people who loved him. Futures. Possibilities. Visions bleeding through time.

Jamo's body jerked back to reality.

The officer grabbed him and pulled him back through the window. Jamo hit the floor, gasping, his shoulder smoking where the Rectifier had touched it.

The CO2 jets stopped. The room cleared. People filled the hallway, reacting to the alarm, drawn by the spectacle of emergency.

Jamo got to his knees and looked out the window in time to see the Rectifier leap across the gap between buildings—a distance no human could manage—and disappear into Detroit's nightscape.

"448, send Fire Units to—" the officer started into his radio.

Brecken came running in, nearly colliding with the officer. He stopped when he saw Freddy. "Jesus!"

Jamo turned around slowly, still in shock, trying to process what he'd experienced. The visions. The memories. The touch that had somehow downloaded a century of watching into his brain.

The jets stopped blasting. People pressed into the doorway, trying to see what had triggered the alarm.

"What is this? What happened?!" Brecken stared at the remains.

Jamo knelt and examined the melted glass globs on the floor. Each one still held residual heat. He looked back out the window at the rooftops.

"I... I don't know."

"Did you see anybody? Who did this?"

Jamo stood, swaying slightly. The room spun. His shoulder throbbed where the Rectifier had grabbed him. "We gotta go."

He walked past Brecken and stumbled. Brecken caught his arm, steadying him. "You okay?"

"They've got it covered. We gotta go, now!"

"But... Rodriguez..."

"He's dead, which means he can't talk. C'mon!"

They pushed through the crowd and hit the stairwell at a run.

Outside, fire trucks and police cars were already converging on the hospital. Jamo and Brecken rushed toward their car, Brecken carrying the manila envelope with the tape and ledger. Firemen nodded as they passed. Jamo kept looking up at the rooftops, scanning for movement, for burning eyes, for something that shouldn't exist but clearly did.

"You okay?" Brecken asked.

"What? Yeah... So Christy believes she has been followed and protected all her life by our killer and it attacks anyone that hurts her. Like that pedophile Father Paul..."

"I don't know that he was a pedophile." Brecken unlocked the car. "I watched the tape. He never touched her that way. He only had her reciting Latin phrases until it turned to static."

They slid into their seats. Jamo started the engine, his hands shaking slightly on the steering wheel.

"Yeah, but she said that her mother recently told her what he did to her as a child."

"If she was so messed up by this priest when she was a kid, wouldn't our killer have murdered Father Paul then? If her story is true? I mean, if he's 'protecting' her, why wait all these years?"

"I don't know... she mentioned that she didn't remember it happening until her mother told her. Maybe if she doesn't know, then maybe he... it doesn't know."

"We're calling him 'it' now?"

"Well, I don't know of any man that could do something like that." Jamo pointed at the hospital. Four floors up, around the melted window, two distinct handprints were scorched deep into the concrete. Each print was massive—easily twice the size of a normal human hand.

"'It' seems the most appropriate at this point."

They closed the doors and Jamo pulled out of the parking lot faster than was strictly necessary or legal.

Brecken kicked aside a pile of empty pastry wrappers. "What are we dealing with here? Are we talking demons and monsters? If we are I don't know if I can handle it. What can do what we just saw in there? I just... this is crazy."

Jamo kept driving, kept looking up through the windshield, tracking rooftops for movement.

"Monsters and demons aren't supposed to exist, Jamo. They're only in movies and books. Not walking around Detroit, cooking people with their bare hands."

Brecken looked at his partner. Jamo continued scanning rooftops with the intensity of someone who'd seen too much and understood too little.

"This is insane. What are we supposed to do? Read this thing its rights and take him downtown? He'd probably just melt the cuffs with his laser beam eyes, that's if the cuffs even fit around his wrists, if he even has wrists... Jamo..."

No response. Jamo's attention remained fixed on the buildings sliding past, his eyes tracking every shadow, every movement.

"LELAND!"

Jamo finally turned. "I know! I know, Randy... none of this makes any sense to me either. All I know is that I saw that thing heading this direction."

"Wait, you saw it? What did it look like?"

"You'll just think I'm crazy and put me in a room next to Christy."

"Try me."

Jamo took a breath. "A big thing outside Rodriguez's room... his—its—eyes were burning... and I think I saw its memories."

Brecken stared for a long moment. "What does that mean you 'saw its memories'?"

Jamo kept his eyes on the road. "I mean it showed me what it sees and I saw it watching Christy and protecting her from Javier and Rodriguez in that alley... and..."

"And what?"

"I don't know. Let's just find this thing."

"So are we just going to keep driving in this general direction until we hit it with the car?"

"No... But this is the same general direction as that train yard where that kid said he saw it."

"You think we're going to find this thing there?"

"Maybe. But after what I just saw happen to Freddy... I don't know if we want to find it." Jamo glanced at Brecken.

"What about the video tape? What were Father Paul and Christy doing on it?"

"It was more like a bible study. After you left, he laid her on the bed, made her recite these passages in Latin over and over again. Then tucked her in and left. The tape goes fuzzy from there."

"Nothing else happened?"

"Nope."

"So what was the passage he was making her recite?"

"My Latin isn't so good."

Brecken looked out the windshield, then down at the manila envelope in his lap. He reached in and pulled out the ledger. The cover bore a circular symbol stamped in faded gold: Divinus septem.

He opened it and leafed through pages of dated notes, careful handwriting in both Latin and English. "Maybe this book will tell us. Full of the minutes taken by Father Paul during meetings with a group called the Viginti Primoris Miles Militis of Flauros Templum, or Miles Militis of Flauros."

"What does that mean?"

Brecken flipped a couple pages. "It's translated into English just below... The Knights of Flauros, the Church of Flauros."

"The symbol from the crime scenes. The fallen angel?"

Brecken looked at the page again. "Everto Flauros... The demon Flauros."

They fell silent. The car's engine hummed. Detroit's broken streetscape slid past the windows. Brecken continued reading, his eyes widening as he processed the implications.

"Seems there was a lot of squabbling going on in these meetings. Father Paul seems to be a moderator of some sort, like policing the group. He makes mention of abuses of power. It also talks about this 'Vessel of Saint Sebastian.'"

The ledger showed images of old paintings and drawings of Saint Sebastian—arrows piercing his flesh, divine light surrounding his martyred form.

"Demons and Saints?"

"Says this vessel carries the hundred-year-old heart of Priest Willem, the blood of Saint Sebastian and the dark soul of the demon Flauros." Brecken's finger traced the text. "Priest Willem is the son of sons to the father, Saint Sebastian. Saint Sebastian started the thousand-year war with the Knights of Flauros after he exposed their church to Caesar in 15th century Rome, and somehow prevented some sort of ritual. The Knights have been battling his bloodline ever since. Until... 1919."

Brecken turned to a page with an old photograph. A really tall priest—imposing even in faded sepia tones—stood with a group of men and women before an old stone church. The priest's eyes held something haunted even through the grain of aged photography.

"What happened in 1919?"

"They... summoned the demon and lured this Priest Willem into letting the demon possess his body, forging a bond that would bring Flauros into a physical being and finally giving the church control over the Sebastian bloodline..." Brecken looked up. "This is fuckin' nuts. Here's that symbol we keep finding."

He showed Jamo a page with detailed drawings of the Flauros symbol and sketches of a shadowy figure with fiery eyes. The artistic style suggested medieval manuscripts, but the images had been copied recently.

"Jesus... What about the passages the priest was having Christy recite?"

Brecken flipped through more pages. "I don't see anything that resembles what I heard on the tape, but he does mention Christy in conjunction with this date over and over again."

"What date?"

"July 15th."

Jamo looked at his watch. The display read 11:47 PM. July 15th. "You're kidding me... that's today."

"He talks about preparing her for what's to come on July 15th and she must bring about The Recollection."

Brecken studied a drawing—a triangle with a girl standing before the shadowy figure merging with the image of Saint Sebastian. The artistic detail was meticulous, obsessive.

"He says over and over that he prays that he has prepared her enough and if she fails the bloodline will run dark for another hundred years."

The car pulled up to a large gate blocking access to the abandoned train yard. Jamo put it in park and killed the engine. They sat in sudden silence, staring at the chain-link and rust before them.

Brecken closed the ledger. They looked at each other, and in that moment both understood they were crossing a threshold. After this, there would be no going back to normal police work, normal crimes, normal explanations.

They got out.

Jamo walked to the trunk and opened it. Flashlights. A rifle with a tactical light mounted to the barrel. A shotgun with similar modification. He tested his flashlight—beam strong and steady—and tossed the rifle to Brecken.

The shotgun felt reassuring in his hands despite knowing bullets probably wouldn't matter.

He slammed the trunk.

Brecken leaned into the car and grabbed the radio. "Calling in our location."

"What are you doing?"

"Making sure they know where to find our bodies."

Jamo walked to the fence while Brecken reported their position to dispatch. The gate was locked with a chain that looked older than both of them combined. They scanned the fence line in both directions.

There—a giant hole in the chain-link, edges melted smooth, the metal resolidified in frozen drips. The same signature they'd been following all along.

Jamo examined the edges. Still warm. "Looks like the right place."

They stepped through the hole into the train yard.

Abandoned rail cars stretched in every direction—rusted hulks slowly decomposing back into the earth. The moon cast long shadows between them, creating corridors of darkness and silver light. No sounds except wind through metal and the distant hum of the city.

They weaved their way through the maze, flashlight beams cutting through darkness, weapons at low ready.

Each car they passed looked like the skeleton of some industrial creature left to die.

They came to a junction between rows of cars.

"Which way?" Brecken whispered.

Jamo stopped. Sniffed the air. His detective's nose—trained by years of crime scenes—caught something underneath the rust and decay.

"You smell that?"

Brecken covered his mouth. "I know that smell."

They looked left at the junction. The smell came from that direction, thick and unmistakable.

"Death. It's coming from somewhere over there..."

Jamo followed his nose toward a cluster of rail cars all lined up in a row. Brecken watched their backs, sweeping his rifle across potential threats. The smell grew stronger. A buzzing sound emerged from the darkness—flies, hundreds of them.

Jamo stopped at a car and took a deliberate sniff. Nearly gagged. "In there."

They approached the closed sliding metal door. Jamo motioned for Brecken to cover him. Brecken stepped back, aimed at the door. Jamo grabbed the handle. Brecken nodded.

Jamo yanked the door open with force.

Flies swarmed out in a cloud of buzzing fury. Jamo coughed, waving them away. When they cleared, his flashlight beam revealed the back corner.

A pile of something. Hard to make out in the darkness and decay.

Jamo raised his shotgun and aimed its light at the pile. Brecken covered the opposite corner.

Animal carcasses. Picked clean except for patches of fur and skin. Deer, raccoons, maybe a dog. Piled like offerings. To the side, a few remnants of organs left to rot, covered with writhing maggots.

In the opposite corner, marks on the floor. Scorch marks. The adjoining walls had been charred black.

Brecken swept his flashlight left and right. On one pass he caught a glint of something shiny underneath a nearby car. "Jamo..."

Jamo turned and followed his partner's gaze. They walked over. Brecken knelt.

A kid's bike on the other side of the car.

"I think it's that kid's bike."

Brecken stood and walked around. Jamo followed. There it was—Jeff's bike, lying next to the railroad tie. The front rim bent from impact.

They looked around. The car just ahead stood open. A bent door lay across from it, torn from its hinges. On the side of the door were burn marks the size of fists. Big fists.

Jamo motioned to Brecken and pointed at the open car. They moved cautiously, weapons low but ready. Jamo hugged the wall and advanced. Brecken covered the rear and flanks.

Jamo reached the doorway and motioned for Brecken to cover him. He peeked around into the car. Dark. No movement. He leaned further, lifted his shotgun and shined the light inside, checking corners.

Nothing.

He stepped away from the wall and got a full view of the interior. Aimed his light at the walls.

"Holy shit."

Brecken walked over and looked inside.

Paintings covered every surface. Floor to ceiling. Wall to wall. An entire rail car transformed into a mural of history and prophecy.

Jamo climbed in. Brecken followed.

The paintings were crude but powerful—rendered with whatever materials were available. Charcoal. Rust mixed with water. Blood, maybe. And in some places, the images had been burned directly into the metal, heat used as artistic medium.

"Looks like a collage. A time line of sorts."

Jamo pointed to small lines under each painting—dates, he realized. A chronological sequence stretching back centuries. As he looked at them, something happened. The confrontation with the Rectifier had left something behind. The walls seemed to animate from his perspective, the static images gaining dimension and movement.

Brecken walked over to where Jamo was staring. An image of a saint with a glowing halo, battling a bunch of men in cloaks. Saint Sebastian.

Jamo's eyes moved to the next series of images. They came alive in his vision—the saint having a son, dying in battle next to his son, then his son having a son, and so on through generations. A bloodline traced in crude but effective artistry.

He followed the images until he reached a line melted into the metal. A dividing mark. On the other side of it the images became more detailed, more personal.

They showed the life of Priest Willem. Meeting an old woman and a young girl named Marybeth. The progression of their relationship. His joy. His love. His ignorance of the trap being set.

The next images showed the exorcism. Marybeth possessed. Father Willem holding a Bible and holy water bottle, looking over the girl who had briefly become herself again—but his face was demented, cracked, filled with fiery eyes.

The priest melting into shadow. In the center of the shadow where the heart should be, a small human heart, barely noticeable. Still beating. Still human despite everything.

Brecken's light panned over the next series. The fiery-eyed shadow following and protecting the daughter of that woman. Then her daughter. And her daughter. Generation after generation for a hundred years.

His light came to an image of a girl who grew to resemble Senator Harris. This girl giving birth to a daughter who looked like Christy. A different priest standing with Christy's mother. Then the priest standing next to young Christy. Then Christy growing up as the mother grew powerful, the shadowy figure hurting and killing along the way.

The shadowy figure killing a priest—Father Paul.

The shadowy figure killing Javier.

The end of the series showed a person in a cloak standing behind an altar. On the altar was a girl who looked like Christy, on fire. Jamo stared at this image, caught in a trance.

"Jamo?"

Above the painting of the sacrifice was a symbol in the shape of a T, with the bottom flared out. The mark of something old. Something specific.

"Hey Jamo?"

Stuck to the wall was a poster of Senator Harris's face—the same image from the billboard. The eyes were burned out, just like on the large billboard across from the hospital.

The pictographs continued past this point, depicting things yet to happen. Future. Prophecy. Hope or warning depending on perspective.

Brecken grabbed Jamo by the shoulder. He snapped back to the present.

"Hey, you alright?"

Jamo looked down and saw his paintbrush and palette—the ones the Rectifier had borrowed. Both had small burns covering them, rendering them unusable. He picked them up, examined them, felt the connection between himself and the thing that had painted these walls.

"Yeah."

"You think Christy might know anything about all this?"

Jamo dropped his paint tools, realizing they couldn't be salvaged. A small loss in the grand scheme, but it felt significant somehow. "I don't know. If she knew someone wanted to kill her I doubt she'd keep it from us."

"What about her mother? Maybe she has enemies that would try to kill Christy just to get to her."

"Maybe."

"You think you want to risk talking to her again?"

Jamo jumped down from the rail car. "I don't think I have much choice."

They drove in silence, the weight of what they'd seen pressing down like physical mass. Brecken stared at the ledger in his lap. Jamo kept his eyes on the road and the rooftops, watching for movement that shouldn't be there.

"Someone is putting together quite a show," Brecken said finally.

He opened the ledger again, leafing through pages they'd already read, looking for details they might have missed. Jamo drove on autopilot, his mind replaying the visions the Rectifier had shown him.

They passed a railroad crossing sign and Jamo recognized it instantly. From the vision. From the future memory.

"I think... man, this is hard to put into words..."

Brecken looked up from the ledger.

"I think... can't believe I'm saying this... I think when I saw the thing's memories, I saw... you."

"Me? What was I doing?"

"I... I think you were hurt. Bleeding."

Jamo turned to say more—

Over Brecken's shoulder, an oncoming black SUV from a side street, no headlights, accelerating—

BOOM!

The impact threw Jamo into his door. The window exploded. The world became rotation and chaos—metal screaming, glass shattering, the sickening crunch of structural collapse.

The car rolled onto its side. Jamo slammed into the door panel. Brecken yelled as his seat belt snapped. Jamo got his head up just enough to see Brecken sucked out through the windshield.

The car continued rolling. Upside down now. Crushed inward. Metal groaning. Jamo hanging from his seatbelt—wait, he hadn't put on his seatbelt. How was he still inside?

The car stopped. Jamo faced the driver's side window, crushed nearly flat.

He struggled for the radio. Finally grabbed it. "216 com... I need immediate assistance!"

Chaos erupted from the radio—overlapping voices, codes, confusion.

Jamo dropped the radio and looked out what remained of the windshield. A large puddle of fuel was forming in a crevice in the street. And Brecken—

Brecken lay a few feet away. His arms and legs bent at angles that defied anatomy. Blood spreading underneath him in a dark pool.

Jamo lost it. "Brecken! RANDY!!!"

Brecken barely moved. Breathing. Somehow still breathing.

Jamo looked back. The SUV had reversed all the way across the street. Engine revving. Preparing for another pass.

The SUV launched forward and slammed into the vehicle again, caving in the driver's side, pushing the wreckage a few more feet. Metal screamed. Jamo screamed.

The SUV reversed again. This time it aimed for Brecken.

"NO!"

The black SUV bore down on Brecken's broken body—

And stopped. Violently. Impossibly.

The Rectifier appeared from nowhere and rammed the SUV with incredible force. The vehicle launched into the air, rolled, landed on its roof, slid across the street and crashed into a wall.

Jamo saw the Rectifier's feet walk slowly around the car. Saw his legs bend. Saw him carefully, gently pick up Brecken and carry him away from the wreckage.

The Rectifier laid Brecken down carefully. Then turned back.

The car caught fire.

Jamo panicked. The flames transported him instantly to another time, another fire, another failure.

A burning building. A woman grabbing him. "PLEASE! My daughter is inside!"

Running in. Smoke choking him. Finding the three-year-old, screaming, terrified. Grabbing her. Running for the stairs.

The steps collapsing beneath him.

The girl falling.

Falling into fire.

Her screams cutting off as flames consumed her.

His own body burning as he clung to breaking timber.

The scars he'd carry forever as punishment for not being fast enough, strong enough, good enough.

Jamo couldn't see through the smoke. A figure appeared looking at him through flames.

The Rectifier reached into the car, bent back the partially collapsed roof like it was cardboard, grabbed

Jamo by the collar and pulled him out. Lifted him with ease and carried him across the street.

Jamo saw the ledger burning in the car—all that history, all that evidence, consumed. He looked at the SUV on its side nearby. The driver's side smashed and on fire. Two cloaked men on the ground. On fire. Heads burned off.

The Rectifier carried him to where he'd placed Brecken. Set him down gently.

Jamo wiped his eyes and looked up at the Rectifier.

The Rectifier looked back. A moment of connection. Understanding flowing between them without words.

In the distance, sirens approached.

The Rectifier turned and walked toward the bodies from the SUV.

"What the hell are you?!" Jamo's voice cracked.

The Rectifier knelt next to one of the bodies.

"Why are you doing this?!"

The Rectifier's hands glowed white-hot. He waved them over the body. It turned to dust, blown away into the night.

Jamo saw flashing lights getting closer. He turned back to the Rectifier.

The second body became dust. The Rectifier stood and turned to Jamo. The sirens grew louder. He paid no attention, continued looking at Jamo with those burning eyes.

Two police cars screeched to a halt. Officers leaped out, guns drawn and aimed.

"DOWN ON THE GROUND! NOW!"

"No! Don't!" Jamo tried to stand, failed.

The Rectifier turned and began walking away.

"Stop or we WILL fire!"

The Rectifier continued walking.

The officers fired.

Bullets riddled the Rectifier's body, each impact creating what looked like a small volcanic eruption. The bullets liquified on contact, turning to molten metal that dripped to the pavement in glowing globs. Each drop left a shiny splatter on the asphalt.

Then with one leap—impossible, physics-defying—the Rectifier was gone. A glow that disappeared into the night sky.

The officers stared in disbelief. One started to pursue, then stopped, realizing the futility.

Jamo dragged himself to Brecken. His partner was dying. Face gashed open on the right side. One arm twisted at an unnatural angle. Breathing in shallow, gurgling gasps.

Jamo pulled him close, squeezing him. "Hold on, Randy. Hold on. They're coming. You're gonna be fine. You're gonna..."

Brecken coughed blood. Made a sound that might have been words.

An ambulance arrived, EMTs spilling out with equipment and urgency.

But Jamo already knew.

He'd seen enough death to recognize it approaching.

And this time—this time—he couldn't save anyone.

The ambulance raced through Detroit's streets, sirens wailing. Inside, two EMTs worked on Brecken with professional efficiency and growing desperation.

Jamo sat by the back doors and watched.

All sound slipped away. Time slowed to glacial progression. He watched the EMTs try to save Brecken's life as if viewing it through water.

One EMT gave an injection. Checked vitals. The other intubated, pumping air. Heart monitor hooked up—heart rate low. Another injection. Heart rate racing. Then flat line.

CPR started. Automated defibrillator applied. Clear. Body seizing. Still flat lined. More CPR. Another shock. No change.

The EMTs looked at each other. Made a decision.

One turned to Jamo and spoke. Jamo couldn't hear, continued staring at Brecken.

A hand on his shoulder. He snapped out of it and grabbed the EMT's wrist.

"He's gone. I'm sorry..."

Jamo pulled the EMT out of the way and lunged for Brecken. Started CPR. Compressions. Breathing. Compressions.

A hand on his shoulder. "Detective, he's gone."

Jamo snapped around and slammed the EMT against the wall, choking him. The other EMT tried to pull him off. Jamo elbowed him in the face. Blood gushed from his nose.

"Detective... please... you're choking me..."

Jamo realized what he was doing and let go. The EMT slumped to the floor, coughing.

Jamo turned back to Brecken. His partner. His friend. The person who had families and movie nights and a life outside the job. The person who had everything Jamo had lost or thrown away.

Gone.

Jamo sat heavily, staring at nothing, feeling everything.

The ambulance kept moving.

The sirens kept wailing.

And somewhere in Detroit's darkness, the Rectifier kept watching.

Protecting.

Waiting for July 15th to run its course.

For The Recollection to begin.

For a hundred years of binding to finally end.

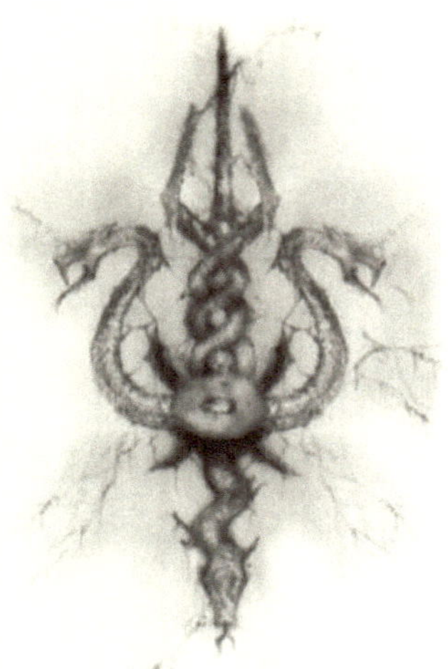

Knights of Flauros

Ex tenebris ad lucem perversam

From darkness to perverted light

Custodes Flauros, filii perditi

Guardians of Flauros, sons of the fallen

Per saecula sanguinem Sebastiani quaerimus

Through the ages we seek Sebastian's blood

Vinculum renovamus, daemon vivit

The binding we renew, the demon lives

In nomine sexaginta quattuor, ardemus

In the name of the Sixty-Fourth, we burn

CHAPTER 6
THE STONE CHURCH

Jamo sat against the ambulance wall and sobbed into his hands. The kind of sobbing that came from somewhere deeper than grief—from a place where all the losses accumulated and compounded until the weight became unbearable.

Frank Dowling, dead of a heart attack at his desk.

The little girl in the fire, consumed by flames while he clung to burning timber.

Beth, walking away with her suitcase and her patience and any hope for normal life.

And now Brecken. Randy. His partner. His friend. The person who had families and movie nights and everything Jamo had traded away for the job.

Gone.

The EMTs gave him space. They knew grief when they saw it. Knew there was nothing they could do except be silent and present.

The ambulance driver turned off the lights and siren. No need for Code 3 response anymore. No emergency to race toward. They pulled up to the hospital sally port with the gentle motion of a hearse.

Jamo composed himself. Wiped his face. Stood on legs that felt like borrowed parts. He looked at Brecken's body one last time—broken, still, gone.

"I should have warned you," he whispered.

Then he opened the ambulance doors and walked away, leaving the EMTs to handle what came next. The paperwork. The procedures. The machinery of death in a world that processed tragedy with forms and protocols.

He had work to do.

And only hours left to do it.

***

Rain hammered down on Detroit with biblical intensity. The Rectifier walked beneath an iron bridge spanning the river, finding shelter in the shadows where rain couldn't reach. Water steamed off his body, evaporating before it could properly wet the ground.

He looked out at the rain falling onto pavement, watching it create patterns—temporary rivers flowing toward storm drains, puddles forming in cracks and divots, the city washing itself clean of the day's accumulated sins.

The Rectifier reached out into the rain. Drops splashed into his cracked palm. The water sizzled and hissed, washing blood from his hands—blood from the cult members he'd killed, blood from a hundred years of violence, blood that never quite came clean no matter how much rain fell.

He stared into the steam rising from his palm. In his eyes, the steam turned to smoke, swirling and transforming, transporting him to another time.

The traveler's meadow. 1919.

A violent rainstorm trying and failing to wash away what had been done there. The inverted cross at the center, the binding symbol scorched deep into the earth around it.

Marybeth was there. Had been there. Was always going to be there.

Father Josef Willem — still human, still himself — had come to the meadow believing he was saving her. The ritual Erasmus had given him. The prayer that wasn't a prayer. The rescue that was actually a trap.

He had kissed her. The binding had taken his tongue.

Fire filled Willem from the inside out. He stumbled backward, fell against the symbol's edge where the sigil blazed in the earth. The meadow burned. The binding completed itself in his blood and her death and an infant crying somewhere in the dark.

Behind him, the church ignited. Not from torches. From him. His rage finding the only target left — the place his faith had been cultivated for thirty years for precisely this night.

They got their wish. Erasmus and his Knights.

The Rectifier emerged from the burning — no longer Josef Willem but something else. Something terrible. Something bound for a hundred years to serve the very people who had engineered his fall.

The Rectifier, returning to the present. The rain continued to fall. The steam continued to rise. The blood continued to wash away without ever really leaving.

He turned from the bridge and disappeared into Detroit's nightscape.

He had somewhere to be.

And only hours left to wait.

Jamo stormed up to the psychiatric floor receiving desk looking like he'd been through a war. Because he had. Bruised face. Bloodstained clothes. Eyes carrying the kind of wildness that came from watching your partner die and having no time to process it.

Jake looked up from his paperwork, taken aback. "Can I help—"

"I need to get in and see Christy Harris. Now!"

Jake typed on his keyboard, checked his monitor. "She's been released."

"What? When?"

"Earlier today."

Jamo looked at the wall clock. Nearly midnight. "Do you have an address?"

"I'm sorry, I can't give out—"

"Well, who took her out of here?"

"I can't tell you that."

"Then can you tell me why a patient was discharged near midnight? Isn't this the fifth floor? I was under the understanding that you needed a signature from a judge before you could be released and how convenient that it's a weekend."

Jake looked uncomfortable. He shoved the sign-in board under the glass partition.

Jamo scanned it. After his own signature from earlier, another entry: B. Harris. Signed in. Visited C. Harris. Signed out.

B. Harris.

Belinda Harris.

Senator Harris.

"Fuck."

Jamo sat in Brecken's patrol car—his car now, he supposed, though the thought made his stomach turn—and opened the laptop. He queried Belinda Harris in the system.

Her face sheet appeared. Professional photo. Conservative makeup. Political smile that didn't reach her eyes. And cautions. Lots of cautions. Any contact with her should be dealt with by a supervisor. Political connections. Protected status. The kind of warnings that appeared next to people who could end careers with phone calls.

Jamo scrolled to her address. Way up near the upper peninsula. Middle of nowhere. The kind of estate that came with gates and privacy and enough land that neighbors weren't a concern.

He put the address into GPS and started driving.

Two hours through rain and darkness. Two hours to think about Brecken. About Christy. About demons and cults and a hundred-year conspiracy that somehow involved a senator, a dead priest, and a thing with fiery eyes.

Two hours that felt like two minutes and two years simultaneously.

***

Dawn was breaking when he reached the estate. Impressive gates. Intercom system. No cars visible from the road. He pulled up to the call box and pressed the button.

No response.

He tried again.

Still nothing.

Jamo backed down the driveway, reversed fifty feet, then floored it.

The car hit the gates with satisfying force, tearing them off their hinges. Metal screamed. Stone posts cracked.

The gates collapsed inward and Jamo drove through like judgment coming to call.

He flew up the long driveway and pulled up to the house. A typical white pillared estate—large but not quite a mansion, three-car garage, perfectly landscaped yard that probably cost more to maintain than most people's salaries.

No lights on. No cars in the driveway. No signs of life.

Jamo parked and headed for the garage.

Breaking in was almost disappointingly easy. He wrapped his jacket around his fist and punched through the side door window. Reached in. Unlocked the handle. Walked into an empty garage that smelled like oil and old concrete.

The door to the house was unlocked.

Jamo drew his weapon and entered.

The kitchen was dark and pristine. Granite countertops. Stainless steel appliances. Everything in its place. The kind of kitchen that appeared in magazines and never got used for actual cooking.

Jamo moved through it carefully, checking corners, watching for movement. He entered the dining room and stopped.

The walls were covered with religious paintings and objects. Crucifixes. Icons. Images of saints and martyrs.

But not the comforting kind you'd find in churches. These were older. Darker. The kind of religious art that emphasized suffering over salvation.

One painting made him pause. A beautiful woman, partially burned. The canvas itself showed fire damage, as if someone had tried to destroy it but stopped halfway.

A small plaque at the bottom of the frame:

MARYBETH HARRIS 1899-1919.

The same woman from the Rectifier's memories. The same face the Rectifier had painted on the train car wall.

Marybeth Harris.

Not just some random victim. Part of the family. Part of the bloodline.

Jamo moved to the foyer and started up the large staircase. Framed photographs lined the wall going up. He stopped, clicked on his small flashlight, aimed it at one particular image.

Younger Senator Harris—maybe thirty—with her arm around a ten-year-old girl. The senator smiling. The girl not. The girl looking exactly like the one from the photos found in Father Paul's stomach.

Christy.

Another photograph showed Father Paul on church steps with the same young girl. Senator Harris beside them. Everyone smiling except Christy.

A sound came from upstairs.

Jamo clicked off his light and moved up the stairs, weapon ready. Another sound—muffled, distant, coming from the end of the dark hallway.

He noticed light leaking from under the last door on the left.

Then he heard something from outside. Car doors opening and closing.

Jamo looked over the railing down to the front foyer. Through the windows he saw three black Suburbans coming up the driveway. Doors opening. Men emerging. Lots of them.

He needed to move. Now.

Jamo headed for the first door he could reach. Got halfway when the door at the end of the hall started to open.

He ducked into the nearest room, kept the door cracked, watched.

Christy Harris walked out wearing a T-shirt and underwear. Earphones in. MP3 player in hand. Moving with the casual unconsciousness of someone who thought she was alone and safe.

She walked to the door across from hers and opened it. Bathroom. Light on. Door closed and locked behind her.

Jamo waited.

The sound of a shower starting.

He cautiously entered the hallway again. Heard sounds from downstairs—footsteps, voices, movement. He ducked back behind his door and kept it cracked.

Fast footsteps coming upstairs. Three men in black cloaks rushed down the hallway. One had a red sash instead of black.

They went straight for the bathroom. Forced the door. Christy screamed.

Jamo charged out, gun drawn. "Don't fuckin' move!"

The three men froze. They were struggling with Christy, holding her while one pulled out a syringe filled with clear liquid. He jammed it into her neck.

Christy looked at Jamo just as her eyes rolled back and her body went limp.

"Put her down. Slowly."

They lowered her to the bathroom floor.

"Stand up slowly."

As they stood, a cloak fell off one man's head. Completely shaven. Straight scars crisscrossing his head and face in deliberate patterns. Ritual scarification.

"Put your hands out where I can see them and fuckin' keep 'em there or I'll add new scars to those heads of yours. Big ones."

All three extended their hands.

One in the back had a hand behind another. He suddenly threw a knife—

Jamo dodged. Fired. Hit the man center mass. Cloak flew off. Blood and brains spattered the bathroom wall. The body fell.

Pain bloomed on Jamo's right cheek. The knife had cut him. Blood ran down his face.

He aimed at the other two.

"Okay, now, all of you slow—"

The man with the red sash moved with freakish speed, suddenly on top of Jamo, grabbing his gun. The other man got behind him, put him in an arm lock.

Jamo pushed backward with everything he had. All three barreled into the hallway.

They fought down the corridor, zigzagging from wall to wall. Jamo head-butted one. Busted the other in the mouth. They reached the landing overlooking the foyer.

The man behind Jamo lost balance and started going over the railing, still holding on.

Jamo tried to counteract the fall, but the Red-Sashed Man made a gesture toward the railing.

Without being touched, the railing snapped.

Jamo and the cultist went over, falling twenty feet to the marble floor below.

They hit with a sickening thud. The cultist beneath Jamo took most of the impact. Probably dead.

Jamo had the wind knocked out, gasping, vision swimming in and out.

Around him, hands clasped in prayer, stood other cloaked men. Scarred. Emotionless. Waiting.

Jamo faded in and out. Saw the Red-Sashed Man on the landing, looking down. Then the man disappeared and reappeared midway down the stairs, moving as if floating.

The Red-Sashed Man reached the bottom and made his way over. Leaned over Jamo, examining him with eyes that held too much intelligence and too little humanity.

"This does not concern you, police man," he said with an Italian accent. "Nor did it concern your dead colleague."

Jamo smiled because he could see past the Red-Sashed Man, up through a skylight in the ceiling.

The Rectifier descended like a burning meteor.

He smashed through the roof and into the house with apocalyptic force. The Red-Sashed Man leaped out of the way with unnatural speed.

The Rectifier crashed into the foyer, scorching everything. Four cloaked men died in two large swipes—turned to clouds of dust and burning body parts.

He grabbed another cultist by the shoulders, setting the cloak on fire. The man closed his eyes, accepting his fate.

The Rectifier threw him upward with impossible strength. The burning body crashed through the roof, landed on the front lawn like an overcooked chicken, let out a final breath, and stopped moving.

Inside, ash settled as the Rectifier turned and incinerated another man's face with one swoop of his blazing hand. Burned another in half.

He turned to the Red-Sashed Man, who had been watching from the side, awe mixing with calculation.

The Rectifier's eyes burned white with anger.

The Red-Sashed Man backed away slowly. "Ottenga la ragazza da qui rapidamente!" (Move the girl, quickly!)

Two men appeared at the top of the stairs, carrying Christy's unconscious body.

The Rectifier turned toward her. Became enraged.

The Red-Sashed Man lifted his arms and spoke in Latin, voice commanding, authoritative:

"Aestuo vis of purgatio incendia, Succurro mihi huic ritus. Per aer quod terra, unda quod incendia sic exsisto vos reus per is ritus."

(Blazing force of cleansing fire, help me in this rite. By air and earth, water and fire, so be you bound with this rite.)

The Rectifier's demeanor changed. His fiery eyes became less ablaze. His hands cooled, as if someone had flipped a switch.

The men carrying Christy continued down the stairs, past the now docile Rectifier, and out the front door.

The Red-Sashed Man studied the Rectifier with something like reverence. "Siete più magnifico di potrei sognarlo mai per essere. Quando la sacerdotessa parla di voi le sue parole non vengono vicino alla vostra bellezza il mio signore."

(*You are more magnificent than I could have ever dreamed you to be. When the priestess speaks of you her words do not come close to your beauty, my lord.*)

He noticed Jamo was gone.

Jamo drove Brecken's car like a man possessed, which wasn't far from the truth. Ahead in the distance, taillights of a black Suburban. Also driving extremely fast.

He was gaining.

No oncoming traffic. He took the opportunity to pass, drawing his sidearm as he pulled alongside. The windows were tinted dark. He couldn't see inside.

The Suburban swerved into him.

Jamo countered, kept it on the road. "Son of a bitch!"

He hammered the accelerator. The SUV sped up, struck the patrol car, then again harder. The Suburban was twice his size, almost pushed him into the ditch.

He barely kept it on the road. His car was faster. He got the lead.

Swerved in front of the Suburban. It rammed him.

"Fuckers!"

Jamo tapped the brakes. The Suburban hit his rear. Jamo laughed—a sound without humor, pure adrenaline and desperation.

Things suddenly got darker. The Suburban's headlights were gone.

Jamo tapped the brakes again. No collision.

He heard an engine blow past him.

Silence.

BOOM!

A pale, scarred face appeared through the windshield. A cultist clinging to the hood.

"PER IL MIO SALVATORE!" (*For my savior!*)

"JESUS!"

Jamo swerved. The cultist hung on, mumbling inaudibly.

Jamo tried to look past the scarred face for the road. Got glimpses of yellow and white lines. Just enough to keep the car moving forward.

He swerved again. The cultist still clung there, mumbling prayers or curses or devotions.

Jamo pointed his gun between the man's eyes. "Jump!"

His eyes darted between road and cultist. "I said jump!"

The cultist shook his head, closed his eyes tightly, continued mumbling.

"What the fuck..."

Jamo started to pull the trigger—

The car hit something hard. A deer.

The gun went off. BOOM! Windshield cracked. Blood spattered.

The cultist and deer rolled up and over the roof, tumbled into the shadows behind.

Jamo cruised in silence, hand and gun still pointed at the bullet hole. Blood drifted up and out of view through the hole.

He snapped out of it when he saw taillights ahead. The Suburban.

He turned the wipers on, slammed the gas, caught up.

The Suburban made a sharp turn onto a rough dirt road.

Jamo cut in behind them.

The road wasn't built for a patrol car—barely a road at all, more like two ditches side by side. The car jumped and jolted with every foot.

The Suburban pulled away.

The car slammed into something big—

Passenger-side air bag deployed.

The car stopped.

Jamo pressed the accelerator.

The car rocked. Didn't budge.

"Fuck!"

The Suburban's taillights disappeared.

He pounded the steering wheel. The driver's side air bag deployed in his face.

Jamo got out, carefully closing the door. A voice from inside: "On-Star emergency, this is Kevin?"

He slammed the trunk shut, grabbed the shotgun with mounted flashlight, and headed into the tree line.

At the end of the path, he came to a fence and stopped.

What looked like an old stone church encased in a massive glass box. Around it, a series of buildings in various stages of construction. All in the middle of nowhere.

The glass structure surrounding the church was equipped with extensive electronic equipment and large tanks. Climate control, maybe. Or something more sinister, Jamo thought.

Guard patrols made rounds at different points.

Jamo noticed a section of fence that had been melted through. Still glowing faintly.

Through the hole, he saw the Rectifier walking with the Red-Sashed Man toward the glass structure's entrance.

Jamo climbed through and stuck to the shadows, making his way to the compound.

Inside the stone church—the same one from the Rectifier's memories—a procession had begun. A hundred or so cloaked followers wearing face masks connected to tubes leading into their cloaks gathered before an altar.

The altar was circular with the symbol of Flauros carved into it. Encased in a transparent box. On the altar, Christy Harris was tied down and gagged.

She squirmed. Looked out at the cloaked figures and saw the Rectifier on his knees inside a triangle surrounded by symbols, as if asleep.

Christy panicked, struggled.

A voice from the other side of the altar: "He would never hurt you."

Christy looked up. A red-cloaked woman stood behind a podium, wearing a mask, face covered.

"He has been your protector as he was once mine... but you took that from me and now on this day we have brought you to this sacred chapel where your protector was born. We've brought him home."

The cloaked followers began to chant.

The woman pulled off her mask.

Senator Harris.

Christy's mother.

Christy's fear intensified, fused with confusion and betrayal.

"We have been awaiting this day for twenty-two years. With the sacrifice of our youngest daughter, our god will be ours again, bringing about a new dawn. The knights of our god Flauros will be reborn!"

The followers raised their arms with a loud, deep shout.

Christy screamed beneath her gag.

Senator Harris looked down at her daughter with crazed eyes and chanted in Latin:

"Vos es reus per meus manus manus. Meus mos est vestri via. Vos vadum pareo meus volo quod meus postulo. Per vox of terra, polus quod subter supter vos mos pareo."

(*You are bound by my hand. My will is your way. You shall obey my wants and my needs. With the power of earth, heavens and below, you will obey.*)

The Rectifier's body jerked to life. Stood. Held his hands out. They started to crack with heat.

He reached toward Christy as his hands glowed white hot.

She pulled away as much as she could, crying.

The Rectifier tried to snap out of it, but Senator Harris spoke the chant again with more ferocity.

The Rectifier was thrown back under the spell, edging closer to Christy, hands glowing and sizzling.

Senator Harris smiled as she chanted.

The followers bowed their heads, awaiting the final task.

The sacrifice.

The end of the binding.

The end of a hundred-year cycle.

The birth of the dark arts would return.

And somewhere in the shadows, Jamo watched, trying to figure out how to stop something he didn't understand, save someone he barely knew, and prevent a ritual that defied everything he thought he knew about the world.

He checked his shotgun.

Twelve rounds.

Against a hundred cultists, a demon, and a senator who could control fire with Latin.

The odds weren't good.

But then again, they never were.

Jamo stepped out of the shadows.

Time to end this.

CHAPTER 7
THE RECOLLECTION

The chanting filled the stone church like a living thing—deep, rhythmic, ancient. A hundred voices speaking in unison, calling to powers that predated civilization. Senator Harris stood at the podium, her red cloak marking her as high priestess, her voice rising above the others as she commanded the demon in Latin.

"Vos es reus per meus manus manus. Meus mos est vestri via. Vos vadum pareo meus volo quod meus postulo. Per vox of terra, polus quod subter supter vos mos pareo."

You are bound by my hand. My will is your way. You shall obey my wants and my needs. With the power of earth, heavens and below, you will obey.

The Rectifier stood and held his hands out. They cracked with heat, glowing white-hot as he edged toward Christy on the altar. She pulled away as much as her restraints allowed, tears streaming down her face.

Jamo watched from the shadows, shotgun in hand, trying to formulate a plan that didn't end with everyone dead. Twelve rounds. A hundred cultists. One demon. One senator with supernatural powers. One terrified girl about to be burned alive.

The math didn't work.

But then again, when had it ever?

He stepped out of the shadows and moved silently through the gathered followers. They were focused on the ritual, mesmerized by the spectacle of their god approaching the sacrifice. None of them noticed the detective weaving between them, moving with the practiced stealth of someone who'd spent a career sneaking up on people who didn't want to be found.

Jamo reached the podium. Senator Harris's back was to him, her arms raised, her voice commanding.

"Vos vadum pareo meus volo quod meus postulo. Per vox of ter—"

Jamo clamped his hand over her mouth and pressed his gun to her head.

The senator stopped chanting. A moment of silence.

The Rectifier regressed, lowered to his knees within the triangle, the fires within him dimming.

A number of followers looked up and saw Jamo holding their high priestess at gunpoint. More picked their heads up, disoriented, uncertain what to do.

Jamo slowly walked backward, pulling the senator with him.

Most followers backed away, looking around, the spell of the ritual broken.

A nearby follower inched toward Jamo. He pressed the gun harder into the senator's skull.

"Not a good idea..."

The follower stopped.

Jamo looked at Christy on the altar, terrified and bound. He pointed to the follower. "You. Get the girl out of there."

The follower looked to Senator Harris.

"Do it or I open up her head like a Christmas present..."

He pressed the gun harder.

The senator gave a slight nod.

The follower walked toward the encased altar.

"This doesn't change anything," Senator Harris said through his fingers. Then she spoke clearly:

"Tribuo mihi vox!"

Give me power.

She waved her arm and Jamo flew off into a corner, slamming into the stone wall hard enough to see stars.

His gun clattered across the floor. He struggled to stay conscious.

"What is all this?" Christy had been freed from her restraints. She stared at her mother with confusion and betrayal.

"Your feeble mind can't understand the magnitude of what is happening, child."

"But I'm your daughter. Why are you doing this? Please, I love you..."

The senator looked disgusted. "And I've hated you the moment I learned I was impregnated with a child that was female. I knew there would be a shift in priority and you would eventually be the next chosen one. I should be on that altar! You robbed me of my legacy that I worked so hard to build!"

Christy recoiled as if slapped. "Why did you have me then?"

"The moment you were conceived the Demon began protecting you... he wouldn't allow an abortion. So, I used you like a puppet to get him to do my bidding... like silencing your precious Father Paul."

"You lied about Father Paul?"

"He was not what he claimed to be... Now, SILENCE!" Senator Harris began the chant again.

"Vos es reus per meus manus manus. Meus mos est vestri via. Vos vadum pareo meus..."

The Rectifier slowly rose. The fires within him gained strength.

The followers began chanting again.

"Volo quod meus postulo. Per vox of terra, polus—"

A loud bang.

A bullet ripped through Senator Harris's shoulder, taking her to her knees.

Jamo sat up in the corner, holding his gun, vision swimming but aim true.

The Rectifier stopped. The cloaked followers stopped.

The senator collapsed but continued her chant through gritted teeth. "P-polus quod subter supter vos mos..."

The Rectifier continued toward Christy.

Christy looked at the Rectifier approaching with glowing hands. Looked at her wounded mother chanting. And suddenly understood.

Father Paul. All those sessions. All those Latin phrases repeated until they were muscle memory.

He'd been preparing her for this.

She spoke, her voice clear and strong:

"Polus supremus quod incendia subter supter, sino cruor of Sebastian mano per is everto pectus pectoris quondam iterum..."

Heavens above and fires below, allow the blood of Sebastian to flow through this demon heart once again...

The Rectifier stopped. Began to tremble. He fell toward the altar, onto his knees, grasping the edge. His hands seared the stone where they touched.

Senator Harris reached out. "No! Stop! Stop her!"

Two followers headed for Christy. Jamo fired twice, hitting both in the knees. They went down screaming.

Some followers ran for the doors, crying. Others stood mesmerized.

Christy continued, louder than before:

"Sino is animus futurus..."

Allow this soul to be...

The Rectifier looked up at her, his eyes full of fear.

Christy looked directly at him and continued:

"Sino is animus futurus universus quod haud diutius permissum everto imperium animus, tamen animus tempero everto!"

Allow this soul to be whole and no longer let the demon control this soul, but the soul to control the demon.

The Rectifier fell to the floor. His body jerked.

"No!" Senator Harris screamed.

Memories flooded back. Not the Rectifier's memories—Father Willem's memories. His true memories. Uncorrupted by a century of demonic binding.

Painting in the church basement. The sunlight on canvas. Marybeth's smile. Real. Human. Before everything went wrong.

Meeting the old woman who turned out to be no grandmother but a member of the Knights. Being introduced to Marybeth. Falling in love. Being so goddamned naive.

The exorcism. The trap. The moment he delivered his baby, his tongue was singed off and he became a prison of transformation.

But deeper than that. Older memories. Not his own but his ancestors'. The bloodline of Saint Sebastian stretching back through time. Warriors. Priests. Protectors. Men and women who had fought the Knights of Flauros for a thousand years.

He saw himself in the mirror as Father Willem. Young. Faithful. Human.

And he understood what had been taken from him.

What could now be reclaimed.

Christy looked at her mother with something beyond fear. Understanding, maybe. Pity.

Senator Harris spat toward her daughter. "You stupid child! Iuguolo suus!"

Kill her.

The remaining followers rushed toward Christy.

Some saw Jamo in the corner and headed for him.

A low rumbling was heard. The followers stopped. The rumbling intensified—like a roaring blaze getting closer.

Two large hands engulfed in white-hot flames swept up from behind the altar.

Several followers screamed, burst into flames, then crumbled to dust.

The Rectifier emerged, fully enraged. Something was different. The fires that burned inside him shone with purity, with ferocity that had been absent before. Not demonic fire controlled by binding spells.

Free fire.

He rose and glared at the remaining followers, eyes burning white with immense rage.

He lunged and grabbed two. They caught fire and were thrown backward into the crowd. Another burning as he was torn apart.

The Rectifier growled as he incinerrated everyone within a five-foot radius.

Another jumped onto his back, screaming in tongues. The Rectifier grabbed him by the head, set it on fire, and threw the flaming body up into the rafters.

The burning bodies began catching the pews, rafters, and floor on fire. The ancient stone church became an inferno.

The Rectifier continued his warpath, disposing of a barrier of followers with two swipes of his fiery hands—

Exposing Senator Harris trying to stand. She fell back to sitting, pushed herself across the floor, bleeding profusely. She looked up at the Rectifier approaching.

"Seal it! Now!"

Outside the encased church, a cloaked man at a control panel pressed buttons. The apparatus came to life. Air vents hummed. A loud hissing sound filled the building.

Senator Harris pulled her mask over her face.

The fires around the church were snuffed out as oxygen was replaced in the room.

Jamo started to choke, gasping for his last breath of air.

The Rectifier's eyes started to dim. He looked down at his hands. They lost their intensity. He lowered to his knees, the fires within him dissipating.

Several masked followers converged on him. It took all of them to budge his massive body. They dragged him through the thickening smoke toward the triangle on the floor.

"No!" Christy pounded on the floor.

Jamo lay on the ground, raised a trembling arm, tried to aim his gun upward. He fired.

Senator Harris's head spun at the sound.

Jamo fired again. Almost unconscious. One last time—

The bullet went out through the gaping roof of the stone church, shattered one of the clear panels in the glass structure surrounding it.

The nitrogen rushing out violently.

Jamo passed out as fragments rained down.

The hands of the followers carrying the Rectifier began to burn. They saw glowing eyes shine back at them.

They let go and ran.

Senator Harris tried to get up, failed. She crawled along the wall, feeling her way through the dissipating smoke.

Screaming could be heard. The senator stopped and looked toward the sounds.

A flaming shadow flew about, reigniting the cindering church. A yellow glow emerged from within it, revealing the huge silhouette of the Rectifier walking toward her.

She tried the binding spell again, coughing: "Per aer quod terra, unda quod incendia... Sic exsisto vos reus Per is ritus..."

By air and earth, water and fire, so be you bound with this rite.

The spell didn't phase him. She continued trying, fear creeping into her voice.

"Per aer quod terra, unda quod incendia..."

The Rectifier kept moving toward her.

The Rectifier stood over Senator Harris, looked down at her, then back at Christy.

Christy could see now. She understood, as did the Rectifier.

"You hurt me, mother," Christy said quietly.

The Rectifier's eyes erupted with white flames as he reached down. Senator Harris screamed.

He plunged his thumbs into her eye sockets, searing and cooking everything around them. Her hair burned wildly as her screaming face bubbled and peeled apart.

The senator's body crumbled to dust.

Just as the Rectifier stepped away, a large fiery beam collapsed over him. Part of it landed near Jamo, who was conscious now and still in the corner.

Jamo panicked. The fire. The flames. The girl in the burning building screaming as she fell.

The church was being consumed.

The Rectifier saw Jamo frozen with fear. He quickly moved the huge burning beam and rushed over.

Jamo was paralyzed. Couldn't move. Couldn't breathe. Couldn't do anything except remember fire and failure — the burning building, the stairs giving way, the child's face in the smoke that he had not reached in time and had been reaching for in his nightmares for twenty years. This was the shape his death had always taken in the dark hours.

Fire. The specific helplessness of a body that could not move fast enough. He had known it would end this way.

The Rectifier stopped.

Not the hesitation of a mechanism recalculating. Something else — a stillness that was different from the binding's operational stillness, different from the directed certainty of a weapon oriented toward a target. The golden eyes were on Jamo and they were reading something that the binding had no framework for reading because it was not threat and it was not vessel and it was not any of the categories the mechanism used.

It was recognition.

The hospital. The contact. The flood of memory that had moved between them in Rodriguez's room — Jamo's hands on the burning wrists and the specific involuntary transfer of everything Jamo carried, everything the binding had pulled from him in that moment of contact. The burning building. The child. The stairs. Twenty years of a failure that had never stopped being present.

Josef Willem had seen it.

He had seen a man who had run into fire to save someone.

The Rectifier blasted a large hole into the stone wall next to Jamo with one strike of his burning fist.

Not through him. Next to him. The wall giving way in a burst of heat and stone, the opening large enough for a man to move through, the air beyond it cooler and dark and clear of the encasement's interior.

The golden eyes held Jamo's for one second.

Then they moved on.

It was not the binding. The binding had changed — Christy's voice already in the encasement's air, the prayer beginning its work, the mechanism's hundred years winding toward their close. What moved the fist into the wall instead of into the man was not the mechanism.

It was Josef Willem.

Making the only choice that was entirely his own.

This one does not burn.

Another large, fiery beam collapsed behind them, shattering the case around Christy. She screamed.

The Rectifier saw her trapped under a burning beam on the altar. He picked Jamo up with one hand and tossed him through the hole, sending him to safety.

Jamo landed just short of the wall of windows that surrounded the church. As he tried to get to his feet, he could see—

The Rectifier inside, rushing to Christy. Just as he reached her, he covered her with his body as the entire ceiling and parts of the walls collapsed around them.

Jamo looked on, helpless.

A hand on his shoulder—a fireman guiding him out the door of the clear structure and away from the burning church. It all seemed like a dream. Flashing blue and red lights bouncing off the windows of the giant case.

***

Jamo sat on the back of an ambulance, staring at the stone church in the distance as firemen hosed the flames. Smoke rose into the night sky. Police cars contained various cloaked followers. Fire trucks pumped water. The whole scene had the surreal quality of a disaster movie.

"You okay, son?"

Jamo turned to see Captain Michaels next to him. He seemed relieved to see a familiar face.

"What are you doing all the way up here?"

"I could ask you the same question. Brecken's On-Star locator was tripped."

Michaels paused, finding the words. "I'm sorry about your partner, Jamo."

Michaels looked out over the smoking compound. "What're we going to find once that fire is out?"

Jamo looked at the rising smoke. Bodies. Ash. Evidence of things that couldn't be explained in official reports.

"I'm not sure... I have trouble remembering details."

The camera pulled back and up, away from the ambulance, over the burning compound, up a ridge overlooking the area.

On the edge of the ridge above the burning compound, the Rectifier held Christy. He was no longer just the Rectifier. He was Josef Willem. He was the demon Flauros. He was both and neither and something new.

He turned and walked out of sight, carrying the girl he'd protected for twenty-two years, just as he'd protected her mother and grandmother before her.

The bloodline of Saint Sebastian continued.

The binding was broken.

And somewhere in the world, someone was watching.

***

A lone TV screen glowed in a corner of a shadowy room filled with audio and video equipment. Two silhouetted men stood and watched.

On the screen was footage from closed-circuit cameras showing the events that had transpired in the stone church. The Rectifier killing cloaked men. Using his immense abilities. Brutally killing Senator Harris, her body crumbling to ash.

The footage ended on a blue screen.

One man turned to the other.

"Find him."

The other nodded, left the room, walked out into a huge, ornate hall filled with religious artifacts. He continued out of the building.

Into Vatican City.

Rome.

The Catholic Church had been watching.

Waiting.

And now they would act.

***

Christy and the Rectifier made their way toward a large city in the distance. She walked beside him, no longer afraid. He had saved her. Protected her. Killed her mother to keep her safe.

"What happens now?" she asked.

The Rectifier—Willem—looked down at her with eyes that burned less with demonic fire and more with human warmth. He didn't answer because he couldn't, which didn't matter because he didn't know.

For a hundred years he'd been bound. Controlled. Used as a weapon by the very people who'd cursed him.

Now he was free.

Free to protect?

Free to choose?

Free to be both demon and man?

And somewhere behind them, in the smoking ruins of the stone church, Jamo sat and tried to remember details he knew he'd forget by morning.

Tried to make sense of what he'd seen.

Tried to understand how the world could contain such darkness and such light simultaneously.

He failed.

But he'd keep trying.

Because that's what detectives did.

They searched for truth even when truth defied understanding.

They sought justice even when justice wore a demon's face.

They protected people even when people included monsters who saved lives.

Jamo looked up at the smoke rising into the night sky and thought about Brecken. About Beth. About the little girl in the fire. About Frank Dowling and Father Paul and all the people who'd died in pursuit of or protection from something bigger than themselves.

"Detective?" The EMT offered him water.

Jamo took it. Drank. Waited for the sun to rise.

And in the distance, the Rectifier and Christy disappeared into the darkness.

Free.

Together.

Watched.

The end of one story.

The beginning of another.

EPILOGUE

Free & Burning

July 2019 — Three Months After

The binding broke at 11:47 PM on July 15, 2019. Christy had felt it at the exact time because she had been watching the symbol in the stone floor of the Ackland ruins when it happened — the carved lines of the Flauros sigil that had been burning their cold permanent burn since 1919, the same symbol she had been told about across twenty-two years of Father Paul's careful preparation and was now standing at the center of for the first time, and the burning in it went out. Not dimmed. Not reduced. Out — the specific absolute cessation of something that had been continuous for exactly one hundred years to the hour from the night Josef Willem had been transformed in this same space in July 1919.

Erasmus had built the binding to last exactly that long.

She had understood this much from Father Paul's teaching — that the binding's century was deliberate, that Erasmus had designed the duration with the specific intention of a man who had decided the mechanism he built needed an end date. What she had understood less clearly, standing in the ruins with the symbol dark for the first time in her lifetime, was the distinction between what Erasmus had intended and what had actually been accomplished.

It was not an ending.

It was a reversal. And reversal, she was beginning to understand, was not the same thing.

Erasmus had started with one design: a binding that would renew. A century of Covenant control followed by another century, the mechanism self-perpetuating, the bloodline weaponized indefinitely. That had been the original architecture. He had built it with a craftsman's precision and a calculator's coldness and he had lived inside his own construction for thirty years before his epiphany had changed what the construction was for.

The epiphany had produced a different design. Not renewal but release. The Vatican as the instrument of a genuine ending — the reversal ingredients planted in the research journal, the bloodline member required to speak it with full knowledge, the binding broken and Josef Willem freed from everything the Covenant had made of him across a century of compulsion. Erasmus had wanted to end the war. He had believed he was building the mechanism for exactly that.

But Erasmus was on borrowed time when he came up with the plan.

And the Vatican had been reading it for sixty years.

She stood in the dark ruins with the symbol cold beneath her feet and she held this thought carefully, the way she held things that were significant before she had finished understanding them, and she looked at Josef Willem standing at the edge of the space where the symbol had burned since before she was born, and she thought: it was a reversal. Not an ending. And those were not the same thing.

She did not say this aloud.

She did not have enough yet to say it aloud.

She stored it in the place she filed things she was not finished with, and she watched the binding's last light go out of the stone, and she waited for whatever came next.

She had not known most of what she knew now, which was one of the specific horrors of the life Father Paul had been preparing her for — the preparation had been thorough and the preparation had been incomplete simultaneously, the way all preparation for things that had never happened before was thorough and incomplete. He had given her the Latin. He had given her the theology. He had given her twenty-two years of proximity to the specific quality of a man who understood what the binding was and what breaking it required and who had died before he could finish the sentence.

She had finished the sentence.

She had spoken the prayer in the burning encasement with Belinda Harris's ritual collapsing around her and the Rectifier standing at the center of it and Detective Jamo's voice somewhere behind her and the prayer had done what Father Paul had trained it to do — not what Belinda had intended the night to accomplish, not the renewal of the binding with Christy as the sacrificed vessel and Belinda as the new architect, but the reversal. The release. The specific theological unwinding of a hundred years of compulsion.

Now it was the Vatican's turn and Father Paul had won.

He had won from the ground of Saint Anthony's Cathedral where Belinda had put him, through the body of the girl he had raised, through twenty-two years of Latin and demonology and the art of moving through the world without being noticed and one specific prayer memorized until it was below thought, below language, below the level at which fear could interrupt it.

He had won and he was dead and Christy was standing in the Michigan ruins and the thing that had been the

Rectifier for a hundred years was beside her and was not the same thing it had been an hour ago and she did not have a category for what it was now.

Josef Willem did not die.

She had expected him to die. The version of this moment she had imagined — in the rare hours when she had allowed herself to imagine it at all — had always ended with Josef Willem's death. The release from the binding producing the release from existence, the hundred-year body finally permitted to close. It was the merciful version. The version that made narrative sense.

His body changed.

That was what happened instead of death — a transformation that was not the transformation of 1919, not the catastrophic violent remaking that had taken a Belgian parish priest and produced something inhuman, but something slower and stranger. The seven feet of him remained. The burning reduced — not extinguished, not gone, but pulled inward, contained, the fire no longer ambient and expressive but interior, held close, the way a coal held heat differently from an open flame. The golden eyes shifted — not to any ordinary human color, but to something banked, the gold present but no longer running on the binding's instruction.

He stood in the Michigan ruins in July and breathed.

Christy watched him breathe.

She had never noticed him breathe before. In the weeks before the encasement, she had known him only as a presence in the dark above her fire escapes and on rooftops — the burning figure Father Paul had prepared her to understand without preparing her for the specific quality of understanding it from three feet away. He had been following her. She had not known this until the alley, until the two men and the specific eruption of heat and force that had saved her without explaining itself, and afterward she had understood — had assembled the evidence of all the evenings she had felt watched and dismissed as paranoia — that he had been in proximity to her for longer than she had known.

The binding had tracked the bloodline member through the channel. She was the last bloodline member. The channel had carried her signal for twenty-two years.

Now the channel was closed.

He was looking at her with the banked eyes and she could see in the specific quality of the looking that the absence of the channel's mediation was registering in him — the specific texture of what it felt like to look at another person without the binding's architecture between them. It was not a comfortable looking. It was the looking of someone encountering the full weight of unmediated reality for the first time in a very long time.

She did not know what to say.

She said nothing.

He turned and walked deeper into the woods and she did not follow because something in the quality of his movement told her that following was not what was being invited. He was not leaving. He was simply going somewhere that was his and not hers, which was a thing he had not had in a hundred years, and she was not going to take it from him in the first ten minutes of his having it.

She stood at the wood line of Ackland ruins and listened to the distant sirens and looked at the dark symbol in the stone floor and waited for whatever came next.

Detective Leland Jamo retired three weeks later.

She knew this because she called him from a burner phone on the day she read about it in the Detroit Free Press — the brief notice, six column inches, a photograph of a man carrying a cardboard box out of a precinct building, squinting at the camera with the expression of someone who has done the necessary thing and is not entirely certain how he feels about it. The narrative pointing toward a scandal that would go unanswered.

She did not identify herself when he answered.

"You saved my life," she said. "In the alley. And at the compound. I never got to thank you."

"Christy?" he said.

"Don't look for me."

"Already stopped looking."

There was a pause — the specific pause of two people who had been through something together that neither of them had adequate language for and had arrived, independently, at the conclusion that the inadequacy was acceptable.

"Paint," she said. "You're good at seeing what's hidden. That matters more than you know."

She hung up.

She did not call him again. His part was finished — had been finished the moment he got her to the encasement, to the prayer, to the eleven seconds she had needed to speak it. He had done what Father Paul had not lived to do and he had done it without knowing exactly what he was doing, which was perhaps the purest form of it. She would not pull him back in. He had earned the cardboard box and the squinting photograph and whatever came after.

She hoped something good came after.

The first month was logistics.

Father Paul had been preparing for this eventuality for twenty-two years and the preparation showed —

the hidden safe behind the false panel in his study at Saint Anthony's held documents, genealogies, maps, an encrypted thumb drive, and forty-three letters from people across the world who had been waiting for someone to contact them. People who shared the bloodline. People who had their own stories of men in dark robes and family members who had disappeared and symbols burned into church floors and the specific low-grade paranoia of someone who suspects they are being watched and has no institutional framework for acting on the suspicion.

Father Paul had been building toward a network. He had not lived to complete it.

She completed it.

Not quickly. Not with the clean efficiency of someone executing a finished plan — more like the specific kind of construction that happened when you found someone else's foundation and had to determine what they had been intending to build before you could decide whether to build the same thing or something better. She read everything in the safe. She decoded the thumb drive across three weeks of evenings in a series of motels she paid for in cash. She read the forty-three letters and wrote forty-three responses and waited to see how many came back.

One came back.

It arrived eleven days after she sent them, from an address she could not trace to any server she could identify, in language that was careful and measured and not quite threatening in the way that things were not quite threatening when the person writing them had decided that a direct threat was less effective than its precise outline. The message did not identify itself. It did not claim any affiliation. It said only that she should consider carefully what she was building and who had built the materials she was building it from and whether the foundation she had inherited was as solid as the man who left it to her had believed it to be.

It said: *He thought he was building for you. Consider who he was building for.*

She focused on that line.

Then she closed it and sat in the motel room with the specific quality of stillness she had learned from Father Paul — the stillness of someone refusing to reach a conclusion before the evidence was sufficient, holding the shape of what she didn't yet know with the same careful attention she gave to what she did.

He thought he was building for you.

She thought about Father Paul. About twenty-two years of lessons and Latin and the specific quality of a man who had understood what the binding was and had given her everything he knew about breaking it. She had understood him, in the months since his death, as a man doing an insufficient thing with absolute commitment because insufficient was what was available. She had understood him as someone who had been given a mission and had carried it faithfully.

She was beginning to understand something else.

The Vatican had deployed Father Paul to raise her. That was the word — deployed. He had been sent to Saint Brendan's Parish in Detroit with Vatican credentials and Covenant oversight authorization and a personal history that Rossetti had selected with the specific care he brought to decisions that would run for decades. He had known this. He had known he was the Vatican's instrument. She had known this too, in the abstract way you knew things that were true and uncomfortable and not yet fully weighted.

What she had not weighted fully was what it meant.

Father Paul had been given a version of the prayer. The Vatican's version — the reversal without the completion, the liberation without the ending. He had memorized it and passed it to her and believed, she was almost certain he had genuinely believed, that what he was giving her was the full instrument. He had not known about the completion. He had not known that the prayer he carried was the Vatican's edited version of the full text. He had not known that the institution that sent him to raise her had withheld the piece that would have made the difference between a reversal and an ending.

Or had he?

She sat with this question and did not rush it.

The man who had prepared for her death in his contingency planning. The man who had structured his network to survive without its center. The man who had spent twenty-two years building something that was, she now understood, not entirely his own design — who had been building within the constraints of what the Vatican permitted him to build while perhaps, perhaps, building something else in the margins that the Vatican had not sanctioned and had not known about.

The forty-three letters. The genealogical files. The encrypted drive. Things the Vatican's careful oversight of his work might have missed or permitted or decided were harmless.

Or things he had hidden from them deliberately.

She did not know.

She did not know how much Father Paul had understood about the institution that deployed him and how much he had been as genuinely deceived as she had been and how much he had seen clearly and worked around as best he could. She did not know where the line was between the Vatican's instrument and the man who had raised her with the specific quality of love that the situation had permitted — real love, genuine and present and not a performance, whatever else it had been alongside that.

The message said he had been used.

She believed this was true.

She did not believe it was the whole truth about him.

She closed the laptop and she let the question sit in the place she kept the questions she was not finished with, and she went back to work with what she had — which was considerably less than she had thought she had an hour ago, and which was still something, and which would have to be enough. Her thoughts returned to Father Paul.

Not with grief exactly — or not only with grief. With the specific quality of attention she gave to things she was trying to understand completely, the same quality she had brought to his lessons for twenty-two years. She was understanding him differently now. The man she had known — the priest, the guardian, the fixed center of her entire childhood — was resolving into something more complicated and more honest in the months after his death. She was seeing the architecture of what he had built and understanding, piece by piece, the decisions he had made and the reasons for them and the places where he had been right and the places where he had been wrong and the specific courage of someone who had spent twenty-two years doing a thing he knew was insufficient and doing it anyway because insufficient was what was available.

He had known she might not survive July 15th.

She had survived.

She was the contingency he had hoped not to need.

She intended to be worth it.

***

Josef did not reappear.

He left evidence of himself.

The first was in late August — a symbol pressed into the asphalt of a parking structure in the city where she had been staying, in the specific spot where she had parked every morning for two weeks. She would not have noticed it if she had not been trained to notice things that were not ordinary wear, and the symbol was not ordinary wear. It had been applied with heat — precise, deliberate, not the random scorch of a mechanical failure but a mark made by something that understood what it was making. She photographed it and filed it as confirmation that he was alive, that he was tracking her, that proximity was still his operating principle even without the binding's compulsion requiring it.

The second was in September. A symbol on the concrete pillar outside the library where she had been conducting research — same method, same precision, different symbol. Not the Flauros sigil. She knew the Flauros sigil from Father Paul's documents — she would have recognized it immediately. This was something else. Something older and less immediately familiar. She photographed it and spent three days with Father Paul's documents trying to place it and could not, and filed her inability to place it as information about what the symbol was not.

The third arrived on a Thursday morning in October.

She found it on the back step of the house she had been renting under a name that wasn't hers — pressed into the concrete with the deliberate heat of something applied with intention, permanent, specific. She crouched beside it in the early morning with her coffee going cold in her hand and looked at it for a long time.

She had never seen him make it. She had not heard him come and she had not heard him leave and the yard beyond the step was empty in the grey October morning with no evidence of a passage except the symbol in the concrete and the specific ambient warmth of something that had been recently present and was no longer present, the way a room retained the warmth of a fire after the fire was out.

He had been there. He had left this. He had gone.

She photographed it and went inside and began to research.

The symbol was not in any of Father Paul's documents.

She established this across two days of thorough cross-referencing — the Vatican iconographic guides Father Paul had accumulated across twenty-two years, the demonological references, the Knights of Flauros materials, the binding's operational history as it had been documented and annotated across decades of careful study. The symbol was not in any of it. Not the Flauros sigil, not any variant of it, not any symbol from the Covenant's ritual vocabulary as Father Paul had assembled it.

She widened the search.

Early Christian iconography. Third-century Roman martyrdom imagery. The specific visual language of a tradition that had been communicating in symbols for fifteen hundred years, the compressed theological vocabulary of people who could not speak plainly because speaking plainly was how you died and so you learned to put the important things into images that could be read by those who knew how to read them and passed unnoticed by those who did not.

She found it on the fourth day.

Not in a Vatican database. In an art history archive — the specific academic resource that cataloged the iconographic tradition of Roman martyrdom imagery across the first four centuries of the Christian era. The arrows of Saint Sebastian. The specific iconographic arrangement she recognized from hundreds of paintings — the Roman soldier bound to a post, the body pierced, the face turned upward with the expression that painters had been arguing about for centuries.

She looked at the photograph of Josef's symbol on her phone and then at the iconographic reference on her laptop screen and she sat with the specific quality of understanding arriving not as a single moment but as a recognition — the final piece finding its place in a construction that had been almost complete and was now complete.

He had carved the arrows.

Not because he knew what they meant in the context she was developing. Not because anyone had told him. Erasmus was gone — the last of his essence spent in the puppet moment he had used to deliver his message before the binding broke, nothing remaining. Josef had no voice in the current anymore. He had only the unresolved pull of something the hundred years of the binding had pressed into him at a level below knowledge — the shape of an incompleteness, a question without language, the sense of something unfinished that the dissolution of the binding had left behind without naming.

He had given her the question.

She was going to find the answer.

She tried the archive access on the morning after the warning message arrived.

The credentials failed silently — no error, no explanation, no institutional communication of any kind. The door simply was not there anymore. She tried the secondary access Father Paul had documented, the tertiary, the two contacts in Rome whose names appeared in his files as reliable points of entry into the Church's research infrastructure. All of them returned the same silence. Not blocked, not flagged, not accompanied by any of the procedural language that legitimate revocation produced. Simply absent, the way access was absent when the institution removing it had decided that the removal itself should not be legible as an act.

Torrini had been busy.

She closed the credential manager and opened a search browser and thought about what Father Paul had taught her about research — that the most important documents were rarely in the most restricted places, that institutions protected what they considered dangerous and frequently left adjacent to it unguarded the context that made the dangerous thing legible, and that a patient researcher with the right methodology could often assemble from public sources a picture that the institution believed was only visible from inside.

She had the methodology.

She had the time.

She had the internet, which the Vatican did not own, and the academic databases, which the Vatican did not control, and the digitized early Church records that scholars across four decades had been placing into public archives with the specific unglamorous thoroughness of people doing important work that nobody was paying attention to.

She began.

The thread was not in any single database. It was distributed across many of them — the art history archive that catalogued Roman martyrdom iconography, the digitized Vatican administrative records that a German university had been granted access to photograph in the 1970s and had photographed comprehensively before the access was restricted again, the genealogical resource maintained by a Maltese Catholic heritage organization that had been cross-referencing bloodline records since 1962 as a labor of institutional devotion, the academic journal archive that held forty years of early Church scholarship including three papers on third-century relic preservation practices that nobody had cited in twenty years and that contained, in their footnotes and their footnotes' footnotes, the specific marginal references she needed.

She followed it for six days.

Not dramatically. Not with the clean efficiency of someone who knew where the thread led. The specific patient accumulation of adjacent information, the cross-referencing, the way a picture assembled itself from components that were each insufficient and together were not — the methodology Father Paul had spent twenty-two years installing in her, now being used against the institution that had given him the curriculum.

She wondered, working, whether he had known it would come to this.

She wondered a great deal about what he had known.

On the sixth day the picture was complete.

The arrows of Saint Sebastian.

The hagiography was familiar to anyone who had studied early Christian martyrdom — the Roman soldier, the Emperor Diocletian, the execution order that went to the Praetorian Guard. Sebastian's own men. They shot him and left him for dead in the year 288, the body left where it fell, the execution considered complete.

It was not complete.

Saint Irene of Rome came to retrieve his body for burial and found him alive. She brought him to her house and nursed him back to health, removing the arrows from his living flesh in the process — the specific intimate detail that the hagiographic accounts preserved with the care of people who understood that the removing mattered as much as the shooting. The arrows that had pierced the body of a martyr and failed to kill him. Pulled from living flesh by a woman whose name the Church had kept for seventeen centuries. Set aside.

Preserved.

Sebastian recovered. Returned to Diocletian. Confronted him publicly, said again what he had already said, refused the accommodation of silence. Diocletian had him beaten to death with clubs and his body thrown into the Cloaca Maxima, the great sewer of Rome, to deny the Christian community a burial. The body was recovered regardless — a woman named Lucina retrieved it and buried it on the Appian Way, where the Basilica of San Sebastiano now stood.

No arrows in the second death. No arrows in the burial. The arrows were with Saint Irene.

And the early Christian community, which had developed across two centuries of persecution the specific institutional instinct for preserving objects that carried theological significance, had understood immediately what the arrows were. Not the instrument of a successful martyrdom — those were common enough, the Church had relics of a hundred executions. These were the instrument of a failed one. Arrows that had been expected to kill and had not. That had been pulled from a living body and had been held in a woman's hands while the man they had pierced breathed back into himself. Objects that had touched the boundary between death and its refusal and had been present at the moment the boundary held.

The early Church did not destroy objects like that.

It preserved them with the specific anxious care of people who understood that significance and danger were not always distinguishable and that custody of both was preferable to the alternative.

She followed the custody record forward through the centuries — the movement toward Rome, the formalization of the preservation networks in the fourth century, the specific bureaucratic archaeology of how objects too significant to display and too dangerous to acknowledge moved through the Vatican's physical infrastructure until they came to rest in the place where such objects came to rest.

The sub-basement collection. Level four. The pre-Constantinian relic archive.

Saint Irene's arrows were in a vault beneath Vatican City.

The arrows that had failed to kill Sebastian.

The arrows that the Covenant had built a binding around for fifteen hundred years — not because the arrows had power in themselves, but because the martyrdom they had failed to complete was the specific theological event that had made the Sebastian bloodline significant, and the bloodline's significance was the engine of everything the Covenant had built. The arrows were the origin point. The instrument of the wound that didn't take. The object that the binding, in some sense that Erasmus had understood better than anyone who came after him, had been built to answer.

She sat back from the laptop.

She understood now why Josef's hands had made the symbol.

He did not know what the arrows were. He had no access to archives, no research methodology, no language to ask the question his hands were asking. He had only the unresolved pull of something the hundred years of the binding had pressed into him at a level below knowledge — the shape of an incompleteness pointing toward an origin he could feel but not name.

He had given her the symbol.

She had found what it was pointing at.

She also understood what the arrows meant for Josef. Even if he didn't.

Not as a weapon against the Knights. As his own ending. He was still burning, interior and contained, still carrying Flauros in the way the reversal had left him carrying it — not enslaved, not weaponized, but present, the demon sustaining the body the way the binding had sustained it. He could not die while Flauros maintained residence. The arrow that had pierced Sebastian's body and failed to kill him might accomplish for Josef what the reversal prayer had not — the release not just from compulsion but from existence. The ending he had been counting toward for a hundred years.

She also understood what the arrows might mean for the war itself.

If the arrow could end Josef — and this was theory, not certainty, the theological logic of a fifteen-hundred-year-old relic applied to a situation that had no precedent — then what remained after him was a binding with no vessel. The ritual that had made Josef

Willem in 1919 required the arrows' existence as the martyrdom's instrument. An arrow that had ended the last Rectifier, used in the ritual's reversal rather than its renewal, might close the mechanism permanently. The Covenant could persist as an organization but they could not bind a new Rectifier without the instrument that made the binding possible.

It was a theory.

It was the only theory she had.

Without them the binding could not be recreated. The ritual that had made Josef Willem in 1919 required the arrows' existence as the martyrdom's instrument. Remove the instrument and the ritual had no foundation. The Covenant could persist as an organization but they could not bind a new Rectifier.

The destination was the same for both of them.

The sequence was what they would disagree about.

She called the contact Father Paul had identified in his documents as the Vatican's most reliable access point — a priest named Torrini in the Congregation for the Doctrine of the Faith, whose name appeared in Father Paul's files with the notation: *If I am gone and she needs Rome, this is the door.*

Father Torrini answered on the second ring.

The conversation was brief.

He was not hostile — he was carefully, institutionally courteous, the specific courtesy of a Vatican official who has received a call he has been expecting and has already determined his response. He confirmed that Father Paul had spoken of her. He confirmed that the Holy See was aware of the events of July 15th. He expressed the institutional hope that she was well and that the Church's resources would be available to her through appropriate channels.

He did not confirm access to the sub-basement collection.

He did not confirm that the sub-basement collection existed.

He expressed the hope that she would be in touch and closed the conversation with the specific warmth of a man who had just shut a door with both hands while maintaining eye contact and smiling.

She understood.

The Vatican was not going to help her.

The Vatican had been managing the Knights of Flauros for fifteen centuries with the specific patience of an organization that thought in centuries — not eliminating them, not fighting them directly, but maintaining the equilibrium that kept the Covenant's activities within parameters the Holy See could monitor. The arrows in the vault were part of that management. They were leverage. The specific object whose existence the Vatican held over the Covenant as a theoretical threat while never deploying it, the way institutions held leverage — indefinitely, carefully, as a management tool rather than a weapon.

Surrendering the arrows did not serve the Vatican's management strategy.

It ended it.

She sat with the phone in her hand after Torrini hung up and she thought about what Father Paul had been given and what he had not been given and the specific institutional history of an organization that had been managing this war for fifteen centuries and had developed, across those centuries, a particular relationship to the concept of ending it.

The prayer Father Paul had memorized.

The prayer she had spoken.

It had reversed the Covenant's control. That was accurate and real. The compulsion was gone — Josef was no longer the Covenant's instrument, no longer bound to run the binding's mechanics at anyone's direction. That much the prayer had accomplished exactly as described.

But Flauros was still in him.

The binding's architecture was still present — the framework of it, the mechanism that had been built in the Ackland ruins in 1919 and that the prayer had not dismantled but had disconnected from its original control structure. A weapon with the trigger removed was not the same as a weapon destroyed. And the Vatican, which had received Erasmus's research journal and had spent sixty years studying it with the specific patience of people who understood that the research was more complicated than its author had intended, had the full prayer.

Father Paul had been given a version of it.

The reversal prayer as Father Paul had taught it — as she had spoken it — severed the Covenant's specific control mechanism. The fear channel, the bloodline's compulsion, the targeting function that had made Josef a weapon across a hundred years of ceremonies. It reversed all of that. It was a genuine reversal of the Covenant's binding.

It was not the completion Erasmus had hoped for.

The completion — the final clauses, the specific theological language that would have dissolved the binding's architecture entirely rather than merely disconnecting it from the Covenant's control structure — was in the research journal. In Rome. In the Vatican's possession for sixty years. And Father Paul, the man the Vatican had deployed to raise the bloodline's last generation and prepare her for the prayer, had been given the reversal without the completion.

Not by accident.

By the specific institutional calculation of an organization that had decided a redirected weapon was more useful than a retired one.

Josef Willem was free of the Covenant.

He was not free.

And the Vatican, which had refused her access to the sub-basement collection, which had been managing this war with the patient ruthlessness of fifteen centuries of practice, had the arrow in a vault and the completion of the prayer in an archive and the specific institutional interest in Josef Willem remaining in the state the reversal had produced — unmoored, burning, carrying Flauros without the Covenant's direction and therefore available for a direction the Vatican had not yet revealed.

She was going to have to take the arrow.

And she was going to have to find the completion.

She closed the laptop.

She looked at the symbol photograph one more time — the arrows Josef had pressed into the concrete of a back step in October, the question his hands had known how to ask before his mind had known what it was asking — and she understood that what Father Paul had prepared her for was not finished. It had not been finished by the prayer in the encasement. It had not been finished by the binding's breaking. It had produced, instead of an ending, the beginning of a different kind of work — harder in some ways than what had come before, because what had come before had a hundred years of preparation behind it and this had only whatever she could build from the materials available.

The network Father Paul had started.

The Vatican access she had been cultivating and that had just revealed its limits.

Twenty-two years of training for a war that had turned out to be longer than the battle she had been trained for.

And somewhere in the October dark, moving toward Rome on a road that was entirely his own, in a manner she could not track and would not be asked to understand, Josef Willem was moving toward the same destination for his own reasons at his own pace with his own agenda — the arrow, his ending, the finish line he had been counting toward for a hundred years and had not yet been permitted to reach.

She picked up her phone and booked a flight to Rome.

The confirmation came back in four minutes. The cancellation came back in seven.

She stared at the screen. Not a payment issue. Not a technical error. The specific language of a cancellation that came from somewhere upstream of the airline — the kind of language that had a government agency behind it, the kind that arrived when someone with the right institutional connections had made a call to the right department before she had finished packing her bag.

She tried a second airline. The same result, faster this time.

She sat at the kitchen table and thought about Torrini's voice on the phone — the warmth, the closed door, the specific institutional patience of a man who had already made arrangements before she called him. She thought about what it meant that the Vatican had influence with the United States State Department, which was not a connection that should have surprised her and did anyway, the way things surprised you when you understood them intellectually and then encountered them applied specifically to your own life.

Her passport was effectively dead.

She could not fly.

She opened her laptop and pulled up the Great Lakes shipping manifest database — a public access resource that the commercial shipping industry maintained for cargo tracking, the kind of database that existed because the

St. Lawrence Seaway moved billions of dollars of freight annually and the people moving it needed to know where their containers were. She had used it twice before for research purposes. She was using it now for a different purpose.

She was looking for a vessel departing from a Lake Erie port within the next seventy-two hours, running the Seaway east to the Atlantic, with a cargo manifest that included the specific category of shipping container that had interior dimensions sufficient for a person and supplies for a ten-day crossing and ventilation that was not dependent on the container being opened regularly.

It took her forty minutes to find it.

A bulk carrier registered in Cyprus, operating under a Panamanian flag, departing from the port of Ashtabula, Ohio in thirty-one hours with a manifest of automotive components bound for Le Havre, France. The vessel was old — 1987 construction, the kind of ship that had been running the same routes for so long that its inspection records had developed the specific institutional fatigue of things that were checked because checking was required rather than because anyone expected to find anything. The crew manifest showed nineteen men. The cargo deck showed forty-two containers, of which six were listed as automotive components with a secondary classification that indicated climate-controlled storage.

Climate-controlled meant ventilated.

Ventilated meant viable.

She closed the laptop and packed her bag. Not the careful considered packing of someone preparing for a known situation — the specific efficient packing of someone who has identified the next twelve hours as the operational window and everything after that as improvisation. The documents. The encrypted drive. The burner phones, four of them, and the charging cables. Father Paul's photograph, folded carefully into the document sleeve. Her sketch of Josef Willem.

She did not take much else.

She drove to Ashtabula through the night.

The port at four in the morning had the specific quality of industrial infrastructure before the day shift arrived — the cranes still, the container stacks dark, the security rotation running its predictable circuit with the specific inattention of people who had been doing the same route for long enough that the route had become invisible to them. She had studied the rotation on the drive, working from the port's public-facing security documentation and the specific gaps that public-facing documentation always contained because the people who wrote it were describing what was supposed to happen rather than what actually happened at four in the morning when the night shift had six hours in and was thinking about coffee.

She found the container.

Climate-controlled, automotive components, third stack from the eastern crane, accessible from the service ladder on the container's north face. The lock was a standard shipping seal — the kind that wasn't a lock exactly but a tamper indicator, designed to show if a container had been opened rather than to prevent opening. She had what she needed for it in the bag. She had prepared for this the way Father Paul had prepared for everything — accounting for the contingencies she could identify and building enough margin into the plan to absorb the ones she couldn't.

She thought, briefly, about Torrini's demeanor on the phone.

About the State Department cancellation that had arrived in seven minutes.

About the specific institutional confidence of an organization that had been managing this war for fifteen centuries and had decided, based on that confidence, that a twenty-two-year-old woman with a dead passport and a duffel bag was not a credible threat to anything it was protecting.

She opened the container and climbed in and pulled the door closed behind her in the dark.

The bloodline had made this crossing over a century ago — had moved between the old world and the new one in the holds of a ship, hidden among cargo, carrying something the people who owned the ships would not have understood and would not have been glad to know about. She did not know this. She had Father Paul's genealogical documents but she had not yet read all of them, had not yet traced the thread back far enough to find the woman who had made almost exactly this same move in almost exactly this same way — hidden in cargo, crossing water, running toward the thing she needed to finish rather than away from the thing she needed to escape.

The names were different. The direction was reversed. The sea was the same.

The container moved when the crane lifted it thirty hours later. She felt the swing of it, the specific disorienting quality of a large metal box being lifted by something she couldn't see, and then the settling of it into the ship's hold and the sounds of the vessel around her — the engines, the water, the specific ambient noise of something very large beginning to move through something very deep.

She was on her way to Rome.

Not the way she had planned.

The way the bloodline had always moved when the doors closed — through the dark, in the hold of something heading toward the place where it all began, carrying what needed to be carried and trusting that the crossing would hold and that what waited on the other side was worth the ten days in the dark.

She settled in.

She had documents to read.

Two objectives. One arrow that would end the war and give Josef what he had been burning toward for a century. And one completed prayer — the clauses the Vatican had withheld from Father Paul, the finishing of what Erasmus had started, the difference between a reversal and an ending — sitting in an archive beneath the city she was sailing toward.

The Vatican had redirected a weapon.

She was going to find out what they intended to point it at.

She was going to Rome to steal the arrow.

She was going to Rome to find the completion.

And she was going to do both before the Vatican understood what she was looking for, because the moment they understood, the door that Torrini had closed with both hands in arrogance would become something considerably more difficult to open.

The binding was born in fire.

For a century it held, first for forty, stalling for twenty, corrupting for another twenty-five. And in the ruins where it began, on the night it was always meant to end, it transformed into something no one had planned for and no one could control.

The reckoning had not yet begun.

The binding will end in — **The Reckoning**.

THE RECTIFIED UNIVERSE
A Gothic Horror Saga Spanning Over a Century

The *Rectified* series explores the devastating consequences of binding a good man to demonic power—and the century-long cycle of exploitation that follows.

In 1919, Father Josef Willem made a choice born of love that damned him to eternal servitude. Transformed into the Rectifier, he became an immortal guardian bound to protect the bloodline of Saint Sebastian—a protection that the Knights of Flauros cult would weaponize for the next hundred years.

What begins as one priest's tragedy becomes a multigenerational conspiracy, as each generation of the Harris family inherits both the protection and the curse. From the shadowy rise of the Knights of Flauros through the Vatican's hidden involvement, from Prohibition-era Detroit to modern political power, the series traces how love becomes chains, protection becomes exploitation, and freedom becomes the most dangerous choice of all.

This is gothic horror that spans generations. This is the price of binding a soul.

This is ***Rectified***.

Rectified: The Recollection

(Available Now) 2019. A detective and a targeted woman uncover a century-old conspiracy. The binding must be broken.

Rectified: The Birthing

Prequel *(Coming 2026) 1919. A priest's love becomes his damnation. Discover how Father Josef Willem became the eternal weapon.*

Rectified: The One-Hundred Years

(Coming 2026-2027) Three volumes spanning 1919-2018. A century of protection. A century of exploitation. Witness how the binding shaped generations and how the Knights of Flauros turned a guardian angel into their greatest weapon.

Rectified: The Reckoning

(Coming 2027) The epic conclusion. After a hundred years of servitude, can the bloodline find peace without the aid of Josef Willem?

About the Author

Kris McKenna is an American inventor, filmmaker, and law enforcement professional whose multidimensional career shapes the authentic grit and scientific imagination behind his stories. A certified Law Enforcement Officer with over two decades of experience, McKenna has served on the front lines of real-world investigations and crisis response, grounding his fiction in the sharp realism of tactical decision-making and human behavior under pressure.

Beyond his criminal justice background, McKenna is an accomplished product designer and entrepreneur. His patented technologies—some approved for integration into Department of Defense eyewear specifications—bridge advanced materials science with practical field applications. This fusion of science, engineering, and operational insight informs the speculative frameworks of his writing, including the biological and military innovations explored in the novel adaptation of *S.E.A.*

As a storyteller, McKenna has written nine feature-length screenplays and produced award-winning short films. His short film *Impulse* won Best Visual Effects and placed in the Top 20 at the Boston Motion Picture Awards, with official selections at numerous festivals including the Hollywood DV Festival. His dramatic thriller screenplay *SCULPTED* has earned high professional marks ranging from "9 out of 10" to "this needs to be made." McKenna's work blends cinematic pacing, emotionally driven characters, and grounded scientific intrigue across multiple formats, including graphic novels and book cover design for other authors.

McKenna is also the founder of **Tardigrade Industries**, a protective products technology company and **Tactician Fragrances**, a creative brand known for its equipment-inspired designs and storytelling-driven marketing, demonstrating his unique ability to merge entrepreneurship with narrative vision.

He currently focuses on expanding his intellectual properties—across literature, film, and product innovation—while continuing to develop new theories, designs, and stories that explore the intersection of human resilience, science, and the unknown.

www.ingramcontent.com/pod-product-compliance
Lightning Source LLC
Chambersburg PA
CBHW032229050726
47591CB00001B/325